THE PECULIARS

KIERAN LARWOOD

A MESSAGE FROM CHICKEN HOUSE

I love the way this book smells! You can practically inhale the strange aromas of stinky streets, rotting rivers and slimy villains. You'll find your nose twitching as the story of the most amazing set of misfit crime-fighters unfurls in your hands.

Kieran Larwood certainly made his mark with this, his very first book. It is really rather wonderful, prize-winning and perfect! We are so proud to bring it out again with a great new cover – and his original title!

BARRY CUNNINGHAM
Publisher
Chicken House

THE

PECULIARS

KIERAN ✳ LARWOOD

Chicken
House

2 PALMER STREET, FROME, SOMERSET BA11 1DS

Text © Kieran Larwood 2012

First published as *Freaks* in Great Britain in 2012
This edition published in 2018
Chicken House
2 Palmer Street
Frome, Somerset BA11 1DS
United Kingdom
www.chickenhousebooks.com

Cover design and interior design by Steve Wells
Cover illustration by Karl James Mountford
Typeset by Dorchester Typesetting Group Ltd
Printed and bound in Great Britain by CPI Group (UK) Ltd, Croyd

The paper used in this Chicken House book is made from
grown in sustainable forests.

3 5 7 9 10 8 6 4

British Library Cataloguing in Publication data availabl

PB ISBN 978-1-911490-21-0
eISBN 978-1-911490-22-7

THE PECULIARS

KIERAN LARWOOD

Chicken House

2 PALMER STREET, FROME, SOMERSET BA11 1DS

Text © Kieran Larwood 2012

First published as *Freaks* in Great Britain in 2012
This edition published in 2018
Chicken House
2 Palmer Street
Frome, Somerset BA11 1DS
United Kingdom
www.chickenhousebooks.com

Kieran Larwood has asserted his rights under the Copyright, Designs
and Patents Act, 1988, to be identified as the author of this work.

Cover design and interior design by Steve Wells
Cover illustration by Karl James Mountford
Typeset by Dorchester Typesetting Group Ltd
Printed and bound in Great Britain by CPI Group (UK) Ltd, Croydon CR0 4YY

The paper used in this Chicken House book is made from wood
grown in sustainable forests.

3 5 7 9 10 8 6 4

British Library Cataloguing in Publication data available.

PB ISBN 978-1-911490-21-0
eISBN 978-1-911490-22-7

For my grandfather, James Larwood

Chapter One

IN WHICH WE MEET OUR HEROINE.
AND A POLYCEPHALIC SHEEP.

LITTLE PILCHTON·ON·SEA, AUGUST 1851

S heba gazed through her tiny window to the seaside view beyond. It was a beautiful summer morning. The sounds of the beach drifted in and she closed her eyes to hear them better. Children splashing and laughing. The cries of gulls. She could smell the tang of fresh seaweed. Her mind drifted down to the sand and pebbles below. She could almost feel the waves lapping around her toes and the sun on her face, almost taste the salt on her lips.

But such things were not meant for her, and dreaming about them only made it worse. Sheba gave a deep sigh and ran her ivory comb through her chestnut-brown curls, taking out the tangles. She always took great care of her locks, brushing and combing to keep them shining. Everyone said she had a lovely head of hair.

And face of hair. And hands of hair.

In fact, she was covered from head to foot.

It wasn't all the same, of course. Her face and body had a fine, fair coating that might be mistaken for tanned skin, from a distance. She could even pass for normal in a crowd, if it wasn't for her other peculiarities.

Her eyes were a deep amber colour; in a certain light they even seemed to have an orange glow. She had a pink, hairless nose − like a puppy − and small, sharp, white teeth. Her hands were tipped with nails that looked more than a little like claws. But when she was frightened or angry or excited, her nose puckered into a snout, her eyes flashed, her skin bristled, and she had even been known to growl. 'Sheba the Wolfgirl' was what everyone called her then, and she hated it beyond all hatred.

The hair and teeth were the first things people noticed, but they weren't the most interesting. She was actually an exceptional girl. Her sense of smell was prodigious; she could follow a trail like a bloodhound and read scents like the pages of a book. She had learnt the mechanics of a range of locks, and was able to open almost anything with a couple of old hairpins she had scavenged on the pier. And by the age of five she had taught herself to read from scraps of newspaper and chalk billboards. She would have read much more, but it was quite difficult to pop into the local library when you were covered in thick fur and worked as an exhibit in a seaside freak show. And that was where she had spent every waking moment of every long day for as long as she could remember.

Grunchgirdle's World of Curiosities perched at the end of the rickety Little Pilchton pier, like a jackdaw on a branch. Mr Grunchgirdle, the owner, was a rheumy, skinny old man with the aroma of a long-dead trout. Besides Sheba, the other attractions were a stuffed squirrel with a carp's tail sewn where its legs should be ('the world's only true mermaid!') and a two-headed lamb called Flossy. They were all crammed into a one-roomed shack no bigger than a large cupboard and made even smaller by their cages, where they slept, ate and (very rarely) washed.

It was a poor place to call home, and Sheba spent many hours wondering how she had ended up here. There had been a workhouse before, where Grunchgirdle had bought her, but of the time beyond that . . . Her mind was empty of conscious memories, except for the merest hints that sometimes fluttered by like a thread on the wind. She sometimes thought she remembered running through a white house, the air hot around her yet cool marble beneath her bare feet, but there were no real answers.

If only there was someone who could tell her something about her past. For all she knew, she could be the Crown Princess of Mongolia, the daughter of a rich and magnificent king. Or maybe a hair-covered parent just like her. Perhaps then she wouldn't feel so desperately different.

Just to be somebody's daughter would be nice.

When Sheba had finished grooming, she carefully put her comb inside the ebony box that held all her belongings: hairpins, some crumpled pamphlets, and a sea-worn limpet shell someone had once dropped on the shack floor. As for the box itself, Sheba had no idea where it had come from, only that it had always been hers. She was sure Grunchgirdle wouldn't have given it to her – the only things she got from him were insults and the occasional slap – which meant it must have been from her previous life. Was it something that belonged to her mother perhaps? Or a gift from a loving relative? Many nights she lay awake, tracing the carved flowers on its lid with her fingers and wondering. Delicate flowers, with five narrow petals, like stars.

Flossy raised one of his heads from the sorry pile of straw he lay on and gave a weak bleat. He didn't appear to be in the best of health, but that was hardly surprising. Lambs were meant to be out frolicking and gambolling, not waiting in a dim shack for customers that never appeared. If the poor creature didn't get some fresh air soon, he wouldn't be long for this world.

Grunchgirdle had spent the last of his money on Flossy a year ago in an attempt to turn around his dire fortunes. But no one visited Little Pilchton any more. People wanted to travel to places that had railways or fast coach routes. The tiny town barely had a road, only a collection of massive potholes linked together by smaller potholes. He could have bought a seven-headed purple tiger and been no better off.

Sheba offered Flossy a handful of oats, but he just sniffed at them and gave her a dismal look. She patted one of his heads. She would be very sorry if he died. He was the closest thing she had to company. The stuffed mermaid wasn't very inspiring, Grunchgirdle treated Sheba little better than an animal, and of course the members of the public – whenever they turned up – just stood and gawked at her. Or ran out of the room screaming.

What would become of them when Grunchgirdle finally gave up? Poor Flossy would probably end up as a plate of lamb chops, and the squirrel-mermaid would get flung back in the sea, but who would want anything to do with a hairy little wolfgirl?

Leaving the oats in a corner of his cage in case Flossy changed one – or both – of his minds, Sheba rummaged in the straw until she found her latest treasure: a five-week-old copy of *The London Examiner*, scavenged from a bin. Hiding it in Flossy's straw was a gamble, but worth risking a splash of lamb wee. If Grunchgirdle found it he would be livid; firstly to find out she could actually read, and secondly to discover she had been outside, ferreting through rubbish, when he was asleep. But she never strayed far from the shack on her nocturnal expeditions. Any further and she might not have been able to get back inside in time if she heard

Grunchgirdle stirring in his sleep. Feeling the splinters of the pier under her feet, the salty wind all around her and the endless swell of the sea beneath the planks was enough. *What he doesn't know won't hurt him*, thought Sheba. Although she wouldn't have minded too much if something else had hurt him instead.

She flicked to the last thing she had been reading, an article about the Great Exhibition of the Works of Industry of All Nations. As far as she could make out between the old coffee stains, it was a magical collection of the most implausible and incredible creations of man, gathered together in London, in a fairytale palace made of crystal. There were giant diamonds, stuffed elephants, machines that tipped you out of bed, pictures made of hair (she found that particularly intriguing), knives with thousands of blades, some revolutionary new engine for creating 'electrical impulses' (whatever they were), and machines that did everything from making envelopes to harvesting crops. If it hadn't been written in a newspaper, she wouldn't have believed it.

She wasn't sure she actually *did* believe it. With a snort she flipped the page, and was about to start on an article about Prince Albert's favourite breakfast when she caught an overpowering whiff of meat pie, whisky and sweat. It was a few hundred metres away, but getting steadily stronger. Someone was walking up the pier. Surely not a customer? On the miraculous off chance that it might be, she hid the paper, climbed into her cramped cage and quickly locked the door with one of her hairpins. She sat on her stool and arranged her threadbare dress as neatly as possible, ready to be gawped at.

This was the bit she was good at: sitting as still as a living statue, muscles locked in place, eyes hardly blinking. She slowed her breathing and let her vision glaze over. Usually she tried to empty her mind as well, but this time she couldn't help wondering what was going on outside.

The meaty, sweaty smell of the stranger was getting stronger. And now there were heavy footprints on the warped planks of the pier. She could smell Grunchgirdle, too. The bony old goat would be sitting on his milking stool by the pier railing, his fishing line cast out, waiting for supper – or a customer – to come by. He had the patience of a brick wall, as the World of Curiosities hadn't had a visitor for four months, two weeks and three days, by Sheba's count.

Sure enough, there came the squeak of his stool as the measly old miser sat bolt upright. *He's seen his prey*, Sheba thought. She could imagine his scrawny heart thudding away in his chest. Maybe a bead of sweat forming on his pasty brow, or even a drop of dribble escaping from his thin lips as he thought about what the penny admission fee would get him for dinner. A carrot, or perhaps even a potato to go with the usual fishy broth.

The poor stranger probably only wanted a bit of fresh air and a stroll down the pier. But he'd soon end up staring at a hairy girl, a wilted lamb and a bad example of fish-based taxidermy.

What Sheba didn't realise was that the stranger knew exactly where he was going. And that Grunchgirdle had finally had enough of eking out a living at the end of the pier.

The footsteps came to a sudden halt. There was a clatter as Grunchgirdle leapt to his feet, knocking his rod and bucket over.

'Good morning, fine sir,' came his reedy voice. 'And how may I help you this lovely summer's day?'

When the stranger spoke, his voice was deep and gloopy – as if it had fought its way up through several layers of semi-digested pastry – but the words were important ones. They would change Sheba's life for ever.

'I've come about the freaks for sale,' he said.

The two men stood in the tiny shack, taking up almost every last centimetre of space. The combination of their unique scents was like some kind of seaweed wine that had been swirled around in a barrel of soiled underpants. It was all Sheba could do not to retch. She concentrated on breathing through her mouth only and keeping her features as wolfish as possible. It was hard work. But she'd do anything for the chance of escaping from Grunchgirdle and Little Pilchton. And this was a chance.

The stranger was a fat man. It was as if an avalanche of pie-crust and gravy had run through a haberdasher's and come out in a dodgy frock coat and a pair of size nine boots. Grunchgirdle would have fitted inside him seven times with room to spare. He was also deeply unattractive.

His nose was bulbous and scarlet, a wild tangle of orange hair stuck out all around the edges of his stovepipe hat, and he was wearing a scowl that could have curdled milk.

Sheba found it difficult to pretend that two very ugly men were not staring at her. She focused on a spot on the floor and kept her ears open.

'Well, she's not bad, I s'pose, but I've seen hairier,' said the fat man. 'That squirrel fish is a load of tosh, though, and the sheep's nearly dead.'

'Mr Plumpscuttle! I assure you the lamb is merely resting. He tires so easily, what with all the extra thinking he has to do. When he's refreshed he hops and jumps about like a March hare, so he does!'

'You can't fool me, Grunchgirdle. I've been in the freak business since afore I could walk, and I know a sick two-headed sheep when I see one. That thing's got a month left at best before it's mint-sauce time.'

Grunchgirdle fawned and whined at the big man for a few minutes more, but Sheba could see from the corner of her eye that his face was set like stone. He appeared to be bargaining. Was she finally leaving Little Pilchton pier?

The very thought made her heart skip a beat. What kind of a man was this Plumpscuttle? She presumed he must run a sideshow of his own – nobody else would want to purchase a pair of bargain-rate freaks – and judging by his impressive belly it must be much more successful than Grunchgirdle's. Beneath the whiff of stale gravy and sweat, she could pick up a hint of gas, grime and coal dust. London, she thought. Maybe Birmingham or

Manchester. What would his show be like? Her head raced with a thousand questions, hopes and fears. She began to feel quite faint, although that could have been because of the rapidly building stenches in the cramped little shack.

'Twelve pounds for the girl and the sheep, and that's my final offer,' said Plumpscuttle. 'As for the *mermaid*, you can stick that where the sun don't shine.'

He pulled a cloth purse from his waistcoat and dangled it before Grunchgirdle's eyes. The scrawny man stared at it, his face torn with indecision. Finally, with a great sigh, he dropped his head and reached out a bony hand for the money.

Minutes later, Sheba was walking down the pier beside the tub of dumpling stew that was Mr Plumpscuttle. She clutched her ebony box with two hands. It held everything she owned in the world besides the clothes on her back. From within a basket carried by Plumpscuttle came a weak bleat. She was glad Flossy was coming too.

She could hardly believe she was out in the open air, in full daylight, for the first time since she came here. Her little furry head was reeling, and she peeped out from the deep hood of her riding cloak with wide eyes. It was all she could do not to leap about screaming with joy, but she got the impression her new owner wouldn't approve.

She felt as if she were walking into a dream. The sunlight seemed impossibly bright. It gleamed off the waves, the sand, the hundreds of flapping pennants that hung along the pier. Everything was so vivid it hurt her eyes just to look. As they approached the town there were such *smells* too. Baking bread and ice cream. Sugared sweets and fresh fish. Ale from the pubs. And hundreds of people: old and young, sick, perfumed, unwashed. She'd never imagined there could be such variety. In between all these were scents she had no name for. Endless new odours rushed up her nose, making her dizzy with the desire to run and chase them to their source.

As they came to the end of the pier, Sheba realised that when she stepped from the last salt-streaked plank she would actually be setting foot on solid land again. She wanted to pause and savour the moment, but Plumpscuttle was already striding ahead. She scuttled to keep up, enjoying the satisfying thump her little feet made on the stone cobbles. *No more creaking and swaying with every breath,* she thought.

She had imagined Little Pilchton as some kind of exotic world. She had pictured shop fronts overflowing with silks and spices, great boulevards where grand ladies and gentlemen strolled in their finery, mansions and hotels in elegantly carved stone. Instead it was a dingy little place with a couple of ramshackle pubs and far too many fishmongers. Sheba couldn't help feeling slightly cheated.

They soon left the town and crested the brow of a hill. A whole tapestry of fields and woods opened up before them, as wide as the sea and every shade of green. Sheba paused to gasp at the sheer amount of space, and then they were over and down the other side. A narrow dirt track wandered along between hedges and tumbledown stone walls, and they headed down it, kicking up a cloud of dust behind them.

They walked and walked and walked. It seemed as if they were never going to stop. At last, when Sheba's legs throbbed from top to bottom, her cape was coated in grit from the road and the sun had painted the sky pink, they stumbled to the top of yet another rise.

'We're here,' said Plumpscuttle, the first words he had spoken to her, and he stomped through an open five-bar gate into a field. Sheba trotted after him.

There were signs of recent festivities. Faded bunting was draped along the dry stone wall, the grass was churned by hordes of booted feet, and there were paper wrappers, apple cores and pie crusts everywhere. Carnies were packing up stalls and rides, and hitching them to horses, before rolling out onto the road and off to the next village fair. Sheba saw a coconut shy, a group of fortune-telling gypsies and a rickety old merry-go-round.

Plumpscuttle waddled on, nodding here and there to an acquaintance, until they reached the corner of the field. There stood a canary-yellow gypsy caravan, with a vicious-looking grey Shire horse between the shafts. Written on the side in peeling paint were the words: 'PLUMPSCUTTLE'S PECULIARS – TERRIFYING FREAKS OF EVERY SIZE AND DESCRIPTION'.

'Get in,' said Plumpscuttle as he chucked Flossy's basket up onto the driver's seat and, with considerable effort, began the laborious process of heaving himself up beside it.

Sheba tiptoed to the back of the caravan, where she found a little door set above some steps. She reached up to unlatch it, then jumped back as it swung open. The interior was dark and musty, and packed with shadows. She could smell people inside — at least five or six. She heard a match struck. A lantern was lit.

In the light a cluster of faces appeared, all staring at her intently. They were misshapen, hulking, wizened, alien and like nothing she had seen before. It was as if a nightmare had come to life in front of her.

Sheba started to scream.

Chapter Two

IN WHICH SHEBA SEES, HEARS,
BUT MOST OF ALL SMELLS LONDON.

ours later, and the rhythmic clop of horse hooves, coupled with the gentle sway of the caravan, had soothed Sheba's terror a little. There were two low bunks, and she sat on one, sneaking glances at her fellow freaks.

A hulking giant, the biggest man she had ever seen, took up almost half the caravan space. He had a shaved head, a craggy face scratched with criss-cross patterns of old scars, and a broad-striped woollen jersey that looked as though it would pop its seams at any second.

Squished into a curled ball, he was trying to jot notes in a leather-bound journal, his meaty fingers making the pencil look like a toothpick.

Sitting on the bunk next to Sheba was a beautiful Japanese girl dressed like a boy in black trousers and jerkin. Her eyes were delicately almond-shaped, and dark like her long hair. Sheba had never seen anyone from the East before. The girl looked different – unusual – but perfectly normal compared to the others, and smiled sweetly whenever she caught Sheba peeking at her.

The bunk opposite was occupied by a mysterious figure puffing on a long clay pipe, its face hidden beneath the brim of a floppy hat. It was only when the person looked up, showing vivid green eyes and soft, greying curls, that Sheba realised it was a woman. She was wearing a greatcoat, breeches and knee-high leather boots, and her left arm was resting on a large wooden box, from which Sheba could hear a quiet rustling. It smelled as though some kind of animals were inside, and when the woman caught Sheba staring at it, she gave her a quick wink.

Hanging from the roof was a small iron cage and in it – arms, legs and tail dangling through the bars – was a young boy with goggle eyes and a face like the rear end of a bristly pig. He gurned and gaped as if his face was made out of putty, and every visible centimetre of skin was covered in smears of grime. Great gusts of stink wafted from him as he swayed to and fro, looking every bit like a bored primate in a zoo. He was currently trailing thin strings of dribble from his mouth. Judging by his look of concentration, he was finding it a fascinating pastime.

It was a bizarre set of travelling companions but, now her initial burst of terror had subsided, one in which Sheba the Wolfgirl fitted quite well. She began to feel ashamed about her first reaction.

'I'm sorry I screamed when I saw you,' she said in a small voice.

'That's quite all right,' said the woman with the clay pipe, smiling.

'We're used to it,' added the giant, not looking up from his journal.

'She's got a bleeding cheek, though, screaming at us when she looks like an accident in a wig factory,' said the caged boy, flicking dribble everywhere.

'Ignore him,' said the woman. 'He's awful rude to everyone he meets, so you mustn't take it personally.'

'It's fine. I don't mind,' said Sheba, although actually she did. 'I am a bit strange, I suppose.'

'As are we all, my dearie. And now you've pulled your little self together, I suppose it's time you were introduced to the company.' The woman leant forward, and with the end of her pipe, began pointing out the others in the caravan.

'That great mound of might and muscle is known as Gigantus, the man mountain. The Japanese beauty beside you is Sister Moon, a master – or should I say mistress – of the deadly art of ninjitsu. None can stand before her in single combat. The unfortunate, ape-like creature in the cage is Monkeyboy. There's not much he can do except stink the eyebrows off you at twenty paces, although he can shimmy up a tree just like a real gibbon when he wants to.'

As their names were mentioned, they each gave Sheba a glance or a nod.

'You didn't tell me your name,' said Sheba.

'I didn't? How rude! I am Mama Rat and these here are my little babbies. The cleverest ratties in the country.' She tapped the box beside her, at which a series of squeaks and squeals emerged. 'Hush now,' Mama Rat whispered into one of the holes on the top. 'You can get a good look at her when we stop. Nosy things.' She gave Sheba another wink, and blew a few smoke rings from her pipe.

Through the air holes cut into the bottom of the box, Sheba glimpsed the twinkle of cunning little eyes. By instinct, she hated rodents. The rank stench made her hackles rise. They didn't even smell like proper rats. She swallowed a growl. 'My name is Sheba,' she said instead. 'Very pleased to meet you all.'

'You come from other sideshow?' asked Sister Moon, in broken English.

'Yes. Grunchgirdle's. At the end of the pier in Little Pilchton.'

'Never bleedin' heard of it!' said Monkeyboy.

'We're from London,' explained Mama Rat. 'The East End. Plumpscuttle takes his show on the road for a few weeks each summer, touring the local fairs. That was our last one for the season, so now we're headed home.'

'Thank crikey,' said Monkeyboy. 'I've had enough of fresh air and eating nothing but turnips. My farts stink like a vegetable patch.'

'I've never been to London,' said Sheba. She tingled with excitement at the thought.

'It stinky, smoky and horrid,' said Sister Moon.

'It's fascinating, fun and *beautiful*,' said Monkeyboy, poking out his tongue.

'It's a festering cesspit of horror,' said Gigantus, still not bothering to look up from his journal. 'It's almost as bad as Paris, and that's saying something.'

Sheba was starting to feel anxious. 'Is Mr Plumpscuttle a nice boss?' she asked, looking to change the subject.

There was a mixture of snorts, coughs and splutters from around the caravan.

'That depends on whether you like being insulted, spat at, half starved, made to live in a dismal slum and paraded in front of slack-jawed dimwits night after night. If the answer is yes, then he's the greatest boss in the world,' said Gigantus with a scowl.

'He's a revolting tub of whale guts,' said Monkeyboy.

'He very nasty man. Smell almost bad as Monkeyboy.'

Sheba wished she had never asked. Perhaps she would have been better off staying with fishy old Grunchgirdle . . .

'Oh hush yourselves!' Mama Rat said, glaring around the caravan. 'You're starting to worry the poor girl.' She leant forward on the bunk. 'The truth is, my dearie, that Gideon Plumpscuttle is a deeply horrible specimen of humankind. His soul is an open sewer of self-loathing, which he takes out on all those around him. He is as unpleasant to be around as he is to look at, but . . . there are worse owners, as I suspect you already know. He manages to keep us fed and housed, and he has yet to lay a hand on any of us . . .'

'If he ever does, I'll pound his head into a pancake,' muttered Gigantus.

'. . . and for the most part, he is hardly ever around. He heads out to the inns and pie shops directly after every show, spends all night – and all our takings – eating himself stupid, and then wastes the whole of the next day sleeping it off. And if you know how to handle him, he's a big pussycat.'

'To you, maybe,' said Gigantus.

'It true,' added Sister Moon. 'We have time to ourselves. Plumpscuttle not mind what we do, if we stay in house.'

Monkeyboy pressed his face to the bars of his cage. 'Sitting around all day is dull as stinky ditchwater.'

'That's because you haven't found a worthwhile pursuit to occupy your mind,' said Gigantus, looking over the top of his journal.

'Actually, I think you'll find I have discovered a more than worthwhile pursuit.' Monkeyboy looked down at Sheba and gave her a crooked smile. 'I've taught myself to burp the National Anthem. Want to hear it?'

'Um, maybe another time,' Sheba said, catching sight of the others frantically shaking their heads. 'But I would have thought there were hundreds of things to do in

London. Sights to see, things to learn . . . and all the *people.'*

'All the unwashed street scum, you mean?'

'That's rich, coming from you, Monkey,' said Gigantus.

'Isn't London full of gentlefolk and royalty?' Sheba asked. She had imagined crowds of beautiful people popping in and out of Buckingham Palace for tea.

'It have many poor people,' said Sister Moon, after Monkeyboy had stopped cackling. 'Some very, very unfortunate.'

There was silence for a moment, as Sheba adjusted her mental image of the big city. *Maybe it really isn't such a great place after all,* she thought, *even if it has got crystal palaces and whatnot.*

'Well, it's lovely to meet you, Sheba,' said Mama Rat. 'I'm sure we'll all get along. But now, I think, it's time for bed.'

With a mixture of grunts and cackles, the strange group began to ready themselves for sleep. Monkeyboy wriggled around in his cramped cage until he was somehow lying on his back. Mama Rat rested her head against her box of rats. Gigantus simply stretched himself out on the floor. Sister Moon curled at one end of Sheba's bunk.

Someone blew out the lantern, and the caravan was plunged into darkness, except for the glow of moonlight through its single, tiny window.

'Night, all,' said Mama Rat, and there was a chorus of replies. Not long after, a range of snores began: deep and rumbling; smoky and wheezy; snorting and filthy. Sheba thought she could place them all. In the darkness, a voice came from the end of the bunk.

'You all right, Sheba?' It was Sister Moon.

'I'm not sure,' she replied. 'I mean, I think so. It's a lot to take in.'

'I felt same when I first join show. Now I glad to be here. You be fine, do not worry.'

'Sister, can I ask you something?' There was a soft rustling sound, which may have been Sister Moon nodding. Sheba carried on. 'The others and I, we all look . . . strange somehow. But you're . . . *normal*. Aren't you?'

In answer, Sister Moon moved so that her face was caught in the moonlight. She motioned Sheba closer, then closer still, until she was staring deep into her eyes. They looked completely ordinary, just like the rest of her.

Then Sister Moon flicked the lucifer match she held in her hand. There was a sudden flare in the dark caravan, and that was when Sheba saw it.

Moon's pupils shrank, the way everyone's do when the light changes suddenly. Except they didn't shrink to dots. Instead they became vertical slits, just like the eyes of a cat.

As the light died down, Sheba noticed that Sister Moon was smiling.

'Good night, Sheba,' she said. Then she blew out the match, and disappeared into the darkness.

Sheba lay awake for a very long time.

When grey morning light stirred Sheba, it took her a moment to realise where she was. Her sleepy brain expected her to be in her cage on the end of the pier. But instead of the fresh smell of the sea her nose was full of . . . *the worst smell in the world*. It was stronger than Mama Rat's stale pipe smoke, or the ratty stink that came from her wooden box, stronger even than the baked-sewage stench of Monkeyboy's unwashed trousers, and it was coming from *outside* the caravan.

She stood on her bunk and quietly, so as not to wake the others, levered open the tiny window. It didn't reveal much except a view of the passing hedgerow, the grey Shire horse stomping moodily, and Plumpscuttle dozing on the driving board, wobbling like a giant caramel pudding. Sheba wriggled her head and shoulders through the window to see more.

Fields and woodland stretched ahead of them, broken here and there by small clusters of houses. It looked almost exactly like the countryside she had trudged through with Plumpscuttle the day before — except for a sooty smudge on the horizon. A giant storm must be brewing; great billows of grey and black clouds were boiling in the air. But as Sheba peered towards it, she could make out buildings and church spires amongst the blackness.

Then she realised what she was looking at.

London.

That enormous span of smoke and stone was just *one* city, a colossal sprawl. Thousands upon thousands of buildings, and all of them filled with people. She had never imagined so many human beings could be in existence. It couldn't be natural. Her jaw hung open as she imagined the amount of brick, stone and wood needed to build such a thing. How could there be enough food in the world for all the hungry mouths inside it? How would they get rid of all their waste?

The source of the atrocious stench suddenly became clear. Raw sewage.

Sheba remained stuck, half-in half-out of the window, for the next hour. Little country houses began to roll past, wattle-and-daub lean-tos with threads of white smoke drifting from the chimneys. The view of London began to become clearer. There was a hint of a great domed building that must be St Paul's Cathedral. She squinted closer, trying to get a glimpse of sparkling glass that might be the fabled Crystal Palace of the Exhibition.

Soon there were clusters of houses, then small hamlets with their own inns and churches, followed by the junk mountains. Great heaps of rubbish and manure up to ten metres high, each with a gaggle of rag-clad paupers climbing and rummaging amongst them. They passed the first factory she had ever seen, a shambling cube of red brick with rows of tiny windows. Then there were breweries, slaughterhouses, tanneries and foundries. Each had at least one chimney; all were belching out masses of black fumes. The stink stuck in her throat, burnt her lungs and made her cough violently. Lines of tattered workers turned to gawk at the strange, choking, hairy thing hanging out of the yellow caravan.

Sheba's sensitive nose was reeling. Not only was she

smelling new odours at an alarming rate, she was taking them in at intensities her delicate system had never experienced before. Her coughing turned to retching and her head began to spin. Clumps of black soot drifted into her face and flecked her hair. She tried to pull herself back into the caravan, away from the overpowering stench, but she was stuck fast.

Then a pair of massive hands closed around her ankles and yanked her inside. Through stinging eyes, she noticed all the Peculiars were awake now, although there seemed to be lots more of them. Fifteen at least.

She tried to form words, but she was so light-headed and full of fumes she could barely think. 'The smell . . .' she managed to say, before she collapsed onto the bunk, unconscious.

'Well,' said Monkeyboy, looking down from his cage. 'I know London doesn't have the nicest pong in the world, but there's no need for that sort of performance.'

It was late morning when Sheba came to. Thankfully, her brain seemed to have used the time to adjust itself to London's stench. She could still smell layer upon layer of sewage, coal, smoke, gas, rotting meat, blocked drains and a hundred other offensive odours, but they had been dimmed to background noise. Her nose thrummed but it no longer felt as if it was about to explode.

She lay on a pile of tatty blankets in a small, square room with plaster crumbling off the walls and a window that looked out onto a street of squashed little houses, pavements thronged with people. Around her were a collection of other beds and the box that held Mama Rat's 'babbies'. Tiny rodent snores drifted from within. Someone had placed her little ebony box by her side. A quick check told her everything was still in its place.

At one end of the room was a door from which deeply strange noises were leaking. It sounded as if a herd of pigs was trying to gargle syrup. By the smell, she supposed it was Plumpscuttle, fast asleep and snoring.

At the other end of the room was a staircase. She padded down it, emerging into an almost bare parlour with a small fireplace and a single rickety armchair. Next door was a kitchen with a splintered table and chairs fashioned out of old tea crates. The window was open, but Sheba was too small to see over the sill. Instead, she opened the back door and stepped out to see a bizarre sight.

In the far corner of a dusty fenced yard was the yellow caravan. The opposite corner held a small privy shed and a squat iron cage from which Monkeyboy's face was currently peeping. A gate hung from rusty hinges and on it, in flourishing but faded script, Sheba read, 'PLUMPSCUTTLE'S PECULIARS: A COLLECTION OF THE HIDEOUS, HORRID AND HUMUNGOUS. TERROR AND AMAZEMENT AWAIT YOU. YOU ARE ADVISED TO BRING A CHANGE OF TROUSERS. ENTRY 1D.'

But in the middle of the yard was the grey shire horse – and it had a homicidal glint in its eyes. The Peculiars were trying to shepherd it into a stall next to the house.

'Come on, Raggety dearie. Good horsey,' crooned Mama Rat.

The horse gnashed its teeth in her direction, and she skipped backwards. Sheba hadn't seen many horses, but she was pretty sure they weren't supposed to scowl like that.

'Do not get too close,' warned Sister Moon. She was poised just outside the horse's striking distance, ready to leap to safety.

'Get in the stall, you manky old nag, or I'll pound you into glue,' said Gigantus, bravely, but even he was keeping well away from the horse's back hooves.

Raggety made a deep rumbling noise that sounded almost like a growl.

Sheba took a handful of sugar from the bowl on the kitchen windowsill and walked slowly forwards, holding out her hand. 'Here, Raggety,' she whispered. She didn't know much about animals – except for Flossy, of course – but she guessed shouting at them wouldn't be very effective. All creatures responded better to kindness, she reasoned. That, and a spot of bribery.

The horse eyed her offering, then edged forward and nibbled at the sugar. Despite looking as though he wanted to eat her hand as well, he was surprisingly gentle. He crunched the sweet granules thoughtfully.

Sheba backed into the stall. 'Come on, Raggety, there's a good boy.'

Whickering under his breath, the horse clopped towards her. He knew he was being tricked, but it would be worth it for more of that delicious white stuff.

When Raggety was in the stall and Gigantus had closed the gate, Sheba fed him the rest of the sugar, then clambered out. She noticed Flossy's basket was standing nearby. She guessed he was going to live in the stall, too. He gave her a little double-bleat, and she knelt to give his heads a reassuring pat. The journey to London seemed to have perked him up a bit, although maybe he was just relieved to get away from Grunchgirdle. Hopefully he would be happier in his new home. As long as Raggety didn't squish him into jelly.

'Well done, Sheba!' said Mama Rat, slapping her on the back.

Sheba felt a strange, warm feeling tingle through her. It was the first time she had ever helped anyone, and it felt surprisingly good.

'Aye, that would have taken us hours,' said Gigantus.

'Do you feel better now?' asked Sister Moon. For the first time, Sheba noticed she had two long, thin sword scabbards strapped to her back.

'Yes, thank you,' said Sheba. 'It's just this place . . . this city. I've never smelt anything like it.'

'Make sure you steer clear of Monkeyboy on a hot day, then,' said Gigantus.

A muffled stream of insults began to pour from the little cage in the corner, but they were cut off by a deafening, gargling snort from the upstairs window.

'Come on, you lot, there's work to do before Plumpscuttle wakes up,' said Mama Rat.

'What kind of work?' Sheba asked.

Gigantus pointed to a stack of rope and sheets and paper lanterns. 'We've got to get that lot up by sundown.'

'And then what?' asked Sheba.

'Showtime,' said Sister Moon, smiling.

Chapter Three

IN WHICH SHEBA MEETS HER PUBLIC.

Night fell on the city. Gas lamps lit the streets with a flickering yellow glow, and orange candlelight twinkled in every window. Peeking out of the bedroom window, cautiously in case anyone below might spot her, Sheba looked down on a scene of enchantment. Brick Lane had been transformed into a fairy city (as long as you didn't breathe through your nose).

The pavements were full of ballad singers, jugglers, stilt-walkers and hawkers selling dubious-looking pies — some still with the odd feather or tail poking out. Amongst them milled tatty locals and many grander folk who must have wandered down from the city to sample the slums for their amusement. These were prime targets for the hordes of little pickpockets, who scurried like ants through the crowd, dipping for purses, watches and silk handkerchiefs.

This, thought Sheba, was how she had imagined a city to be, all those years she was shut up at Grunchgirdle's. A place full of noise and bustle and life. The sight was over-whelming, intimidating but, most of all, exciting. Just as fascinating as Monkeyboy had said it would be.

The front door to the Peculiars' house was wide open with signs propped outside, proclaiming the wonders within. Plumpscuttle's morose nephew, Phineas, stood with a money box and a roll of tickets, beckoning in punters without any enthusiasm.

Inside, the Peculiars had been busy. A hard afternoon's work hanging sheets from ceilings had turned the dingy little rooms into a series of chambers. The many-coloured paper lanterns gave the place an eerie, otherworldly glow.

Sheba could hear Plumpscuttle in the parlour. Having slept off his long night of travel, he was letting rip with a mighty spiel about the glories of his sideshow. Sheba peeked down the staircase. He was standing on a box, his ginger hair seeming to glow orange and set off by his ruddy cheeks, which were throbbing like two beet-roots. He only had a small crowd, but he was giving it his all.

Behind him, Mama Rat had arranged the contents of her box into a miniature Big Top. There were tiny trapezes, a tightrope, hoops and tunnels, all painted in bright lozenges of red and yellow. Waiting in the wings were six huge rats. Sheba now knew they were called Bartholomew, Matthew, Judas, Thaddeus, Simon and Peter, although, technically, the last two were girls. They'd all been crammed into hand-sewn miniature circus outfits: clowns, acrobats and even a ringmaster, with yellow teeth, glittering eyes and thick, scaly tails. As the punters gathered around, they tumbled out into the circus ring and began performing a range of tricks. At the merest nod or wink from Mama Rat they turned somersaults, did backflips and balanced atop one another in a teetering pyramid.

In the partition behind her, Sister Moon soon had a crowd of seven or more. They gasped as she sliced the burning wicks from six candles with a sweep of her long, thin swords, leaving the tallows standing without so much as a wobble. They shouted in delight as she sent ten throwing stars into the tiny bullseye of a target. They screamed as she disappeared into the shadows, then emerged behind them and tapped them on the shoulder. They tutted in disapproval as she removed her mask and they saw she was a girl. Young women should be doing needlework, not swordwork. What was the world coming to?

Sheba couldn't gawk for long. The next stop for the punters was her corner of the bedroom. She dashed back and sat patiently on her stool as a column of people filed slowly past. She tried not to listen as they made noises of disgust or horror, and instead concentrated on her own act: being as wolfish as possible. She widened her eyes so they glinted orange in the lantern light, and let her sharp little teeth poke out. But it was a while since she'd had to sit for a customer, and it was hard to listen to their comments after the applause for Mama Rat and Sister Moon: 'Poor thing!' 'What a sight!' and 'Do you think she combs her face?' She'd moved halfway across the country, but her life had changed very little.

Out in the yard, Sheba could hear gasps of amazement as Gigantus lifted a wooden bench. It happened to have three men sitting on it, and he hoisted it over his head as if it were a sack of feathers. She didn't hear anyone calling him names.

Behind his colossal shoulders was Monkeyboy's cage. They had put a sign outside, warning ladies not to approach, for fear of being mortally offended. The few people who had dared to wander over were being liberally insulted and sworn at. He'd told Sheba earlier that he also had a few juicy samples of horse manure to hurl, and he was hoping for someone in an expensive suit that he could ruin. She hadn't heard any screams of horror yet, so he must not have found the right victim.

Flossy was also out there somewhere. On display in his pen for people to prod, poke and stare at. She hoped he was all right. At least Raggety would be near, ready to chomp off the fingers of anyone who got too close.

During a quiet moment, Sister Moon popped her head around the sheet partition.

'Is your show going well, Sheba?'

Sheba nodded, smiling back. It was the first time anyone had ever checked on her during a performance. For once she felt like she wasn't completely on her own. Others were going through this ordeal with her. She was part of something bigger than herself. It was a small gesture, but it made her indescribably happy. She forgot about looking beastly and beamed instead.

The next group of punters was very disappointed.

'What's this supposed to be, then?'

'It's just a little girl sitting on a chair . . . my missus looks more 'orrible than that first thing in the morning!'

'She's not much better the rest of the day, either.'

Sheba strained her hardest, willing her snout to twitch, her fangs to jut, but she could feel her features remaining stubbornly normal. Trying another approach, she instead imagined Grunchgirdle with his bony, shaking fingers and watery, spiteful eyes. She pictured the way he used to poke her through the cage bars with a broom handle, how he cursed at her and called her 'freak' and 'monster': all the little humiliations and unkindnesses she had endured over the years.

It was as if the wolf inside her suddenly woke. With a snarl, her eyes flashed amber and her teeth snapped. From girl to animal in the blink of an eye.

Her audience yelped and rushed back through the sheets and down the stairs. Sheba sat, quietly growling, until she noticed that not quite all of them had gone. Still standing in front of her was a little girl, wide-eyed and clutching at her pinafore in fright, but standing her ground.

'Sorry,' said Sheba. She suddenly felt very self-conscious and ashamed. With a blink, her amber eyes returned to normal, and she hid her sharp teeth behind a pout.

'That was very good,' said the girl. She gave Sheba a shy smile. 'Bit scary, though.'

'Sorry,' Sheba said again. 'I didn't mean to frighten you.'

''S all right,' said the girl.

Sheba looked at her visitor properly. The poor thing was stick-thin and pale as a dead fish. She could clearly see the bones of her skull pushing through her skin, and there were dark shadows around her huge eyes. Beneath her patched pinafore, she wore rags that reeked of stale mud. Her feet were bare and covered with angry-looking welts and scratches. *This must be one of those unfortunate people Sister Moon was talking about,* Sheba thought. *Could she be one of the scavengers from the dust-heaps? Or somewhere even worse?*

'Do you live in London?' It was a silly question, but Sheba didn't know what to say. She'd never spoken to her audience before.

'Yes, down by the river.' The girl smiled again. 'Me ma will never believe me when I tells her about you and the others!'

'Is this the first time you've been to the show?'

'First time I've been anywhere in town,' the girl said. 'I'm supposed to be out on the river now, picking from the mud, but I didn't feel like it. Went for a walk instead.'

Sheba was about to ask what kind of strange fruit would need picking from a stinking riverbank, when the girl took something from her pocket and held it out to her. Sheba looked. It was a chipped glass marble, the size of a small egg and bottle green. Hesitantly, Sheba took it.

'My name's Till,' said the girl. She watched as Sheba rolled the marble between her fingers. 'You can keep that if you like. Picked it up this morning.'

'Thank you,' said Sheba, genuinely touched. It was the first time anyone had actually given her anything. She was filled with gratitude, but guilty too, as she had nothing to give in return. Instead she offered her name. 'I'm Sheba.'

Till opened her mouth to say more, when the thunderous boom of Plumpscuttle's voice echoed up from below.

'What do you mean, she sneaked past without paying? Get off your lazy backside and find her, you dolt! And then bring her to me so I can clout her back where she came from!'

'I've got to go!' Till rushed to the hanging sheets and peeped through. 'If that fat bloke catches me, he'll give me a thick ear!'

'Didn't you get a ticket?' asked Sheba.

'Nah, I ran past that simple cove on the door. Think I can afford a penny?' She put her eye back to the gap in the sheet. The thumping feet of Phineas came up the stairs towards Sheba's partition. Till scuttled under the sheets, past Sister Moon and down the stairs, just as the dozy, round face of Phineas Plumpscuttle peered round to where Sheba was sitting.

'Oi, girl. Have you seen a muddy little urchin in here? Uncle wants me to hit her.'

'Haven't seen anyone,' Sheba lied.

As Phineas stomped off to look elsewhere, she rubbed the chipped glass of the marble with her thumb and wished for the little girl to come back another day.

Chapter Four

IN WHICH A MUDLARK GETS MUNCHED.

Till had been out picking for a good hour. She'd found a few thin pieces of metal, half a clay pipe and a brown bottle with a mouthful of gin still swilling in the bottom. A good morning's work. Enough to sell on the street later for a penny or two, which in turn would buy a morsel for supper.

The handful of treasures clanked together in the hessian sack at her side as she pulled one foot slowly out of the clingy mud and took another step forward. The river bed released a small cloud of green gas, then closed up again over her footprint, leaving no trace of her passing at all. Her feet were wrapped with rags. Too poor for shoes, mudlarks needed some protection from glass and nails hidden in the slime. One cut could mean blood poisoning and a lingering, miserable death. This morning, Till was out with her brothers, Tam and Tob. Three of six children who lived in a one room cellar with their parents, uncles, aunts, a couple of people who claimed they were relatives and a wide range of furry vermin. They needed every penny they could raise to keep them all from starving.

Somewhere to the left she could hear the distant *suck-slop-suck-slop* of one of her brothers, trudging in the same ungainly way. She would have been able to see him, too, if it wasn't for the thick London fog. Usually, fog was just a collection of water particles hanging in the air. The worst it could do was spoil the view, or make you inadvertently step into something nasty. But the London variety was different. It crawled into your lungs like poured concrete, then sat there leaking poisonous chemicals into your blood. It seeped into your nostrils, your skin, even your eyes, stinging and burning and choking. It choked the narrow streets, too. And the whole river, the whole city, was more often than not erased from sight.

Till kept her eyes fixed on the lumpy brown surface of the mud. Her mind kept drifting back to the night before, when she had snuck into the sideshow on Brick Lane. Her left ear still throbbed from where her da had clipped her when he'd heard what she'd done. Not for sneaking in without paying, but for wandering off when she should

- 38 -

have been making the most of low tide. *We can't afford to miss a chance to pick,* he'd said, for the hundredth time. Not that Till cared. It had been more than worth it to see those bizarre people, and to meet that little girl. Just like her, but covered in hair. And those teeth and claws! *If only I had something strange about me,* she thought, *then I could sit in a sideshow like a queen and have people pay to look at me, instead of having to wade through stinking slime every day.*

She was just picturing herself with a pair of feathered wings, starring in a famous circus somewhere, when, out of the corner of her eye, she saw something ripple the surface of the silt.

There wasn't much still alive in the Thames, apart from an eel or two – slimy, pulpy things that were almost blind thanks to the river's pollution. Some folk told of monster-sized ones that had grown fat on the bodies of dead men that drifted downstream, but Till believed none of that. All she was thinking right now was that there might be something in the mud worth eating. Something that would make a change from cabbage water and gruel.

With her tongue poking hungrily between her lips she rounded on the source of the ripple. Slowly, slowly, so as not to scare it, she crouched and eased her way through the mud. Her feet made soft slurps as they broke the surface and slipped back down into the clammy ooze.

When she was above the spot where the ripple came from she stopped and held her breath. She stood motionless for a whole minute, then two. Nothing stirred, and for a moment she thought she might have imagined the whole thing. Then it came again. A shudder in the jelly-like silt, somewhere near the surface.

Till's hands shot into the mud like lightning. She felt the long, slimy body of the eel between her fingers, and closed them around it. Her grip was as tight and hard as the hunger in her empty little belly. The eel didn't want to budge, but she gritted her teeth and pulled with all her might, until her hands broke free of the water. Gripped between them was a fat, wiggling creature, wet and slimy. Till's face broke into a wide grin. It was massive!

She continued to heave, her mind racing with thoughts of eel pie, eel soup, eel casserole with extra eel. More and more of the creature was dragged from the mud. It looked as though it was going to be over a metre long!

Till dug her heels in. Any minute now the head would break free and she could knock the thing's brains out with her bottle and drag it back home for dinner. She started to haul hand over hand, and there was still no sign of it ever stopping . . .

It was about then that she realised that the eel's skin wasn't quite normal. The few miserable specimens she had seen at the fishmarket had been a grey-green colour, as sickly-looking as the river water they'd been hooked from. This one was bright red. And completely smooth all the way down. No gills, no fins, no head. Maybe it was some kind of pipe, but pipes didn't bend and wiggle, did they?

As she stared down at it, a puff of smoke jetted from the end she was holding. It burnt her hands, making her let go with a shriek. She fell backwards, smack, into the mud.

But the eel-pipe was still moving. Even though she was no longer pulling it, the thing was pushing its way out of the mud.

And then she saw another . . . and another . . . ten or more of the things, all puffing out little bursts of steam that mixed with the stinking fog.

'What the hell are you?' Till managed to shout, although it came out as more of a squeak. The mud beneath the pipes was rising up now, as something pushed its way to the surface.

Till started to slide backwards through the muck, her legs pedalling furiously as she tried to find purchase in the slime. Whatever was about to burst out from the river bed, she didn't want to be around to see it.

There was a sucking, slurping sound and out burst a domed carapace studded with jutting spikes. Till got a glimpse of a huge yellow eye and a pair of grasping claws.

And then she was on her front, scrabbling and crawling away from the hellish thing.

Behind her came a cacophony of clanks and hisses, drowning out her terrified screams as she felt something cold and hard and serrated close around her ankle and pull.

And then it was over.

The fog whirled in brief, frenzied wisps before returning to blankness. The splatters and splashes on the mud gradually closed over like a wound healing. The only sign that Till had even existed was her tattered picking sack, and an echo of her last shriek drifting along the river.

Chapter Five

IN WHICH THE PECULIARS RECEIVE
SOME PECULIAR VISITORS.

Breakfast was a cup of weak coffee, served at the kitchen table. Sheba peered over the rim of her chipped mug at the others sitting around the cramped room. Mama Rat sipped hers in between puffs of her pipe. Sister Moon sat with her eyes closed, deep in thought. Gigantus was writing away again, his pen-nib scratching across paper.

'Where's Monkeyboy?' Sheba asked.

'He not allowed out of cage,' said Sister Moon, without opening her eyes.

'Plumpscuttle doesn't let him in the house,' added Gigantus. 'Ever since he did a poo in his best top hat.'

'That was unpleasant for all concerned,' said Mama Rat, shaking her head.

'Is he back, then?' asked Sheba. After last night's show, he had gone out and she hadn't heard him return, or the gargling snoring from his room.

'He back soon,' said Sister Moon. Her eyes still closed, she put a spoonful of sugar in her coffee, stirred it, then lifted the cup and took a sip.

'He'll be in a mood as black as hell, too,' said Mama Rat. 'Out all night, his money gone and sick as a pig. But he'll probably go straight to bed and sleep until evening. We'll just try keep out of his way.'

As Mama was speaking, Sheba caught a whiff through the open kitchen window. Stale sweat, crusty gravy and cheap wine. She marvelled at how her nose could still pick out a scent amongst the London stink.

'He's almost here,' she said.

The others looked at her as if she were mad, but then the front door slammed open with enough force to shake plaster from the rafters. Heavy footsteps stomped across the parlour, and Plumpscuttle's purple, blotchy face appeared at the kitchen door.

'Get me some bleeding coffee!' he roared to no one in particular.

Mama Rat filled and held out a mug. Plumpscuttle snatched it and drained the contents in one gulp, spilling half of it down his front. Then he glowered at the Peculiars.

'I'm going to bed – don't you lot dare make a *sound*.'

His booming footsteps headed upstairs, and his bedroom door slammed shut. A few moments later a sound like a wildebeest drowning came through the floorboards.

'That's him out for the day,' said Gigantus, still writing away.

'How you know he coming, Sheba?' asked Sister Moon, a delicate eyebrow raised.

'I smelt him,' she said.

'I must say, he is a bit on the ripe side,' said Mama Rat, 'but that is a very extraordinary nose you have, my dearie.'

Sheba rubbed her little pink nose with a hairy hand and felt slightly self-conscious. She wasn't used to being paid compliments. Thankfully Sister Moon changed the subject.

'We let Monkeyboy out of cage now?'

'If we must . . .'

The Peculiars headed out into the yard. After stopping to check on Flossy – who was actually making an attempt to frolic – and trying to give Raggety some sugar without losing a hand, Sheba joined the others at the cage in the corner. Sister Moon yanked the door open and stood back.

There was a rustling from the straw within, then a boy-sized streak burst out and began bouncing around the yard, whooping and shrieking. He finally came to rest on top of the privy and gurned down at the others below him.

'Good bloomin' morning, you bunch of sideshow

weirdos!' he said, winking. 'About time someone let me out of there; I'd run out of snot to harvest three hours ago!'

'That is truly disgusting, even for you,' said Mama Rat, which caused Monkeyboy to cackle so much he started retching. After a few moments, he calmed down enough to speak again.

'Right, Sheba. Time for the National Anthem.'

The bells of Christ Church struck four in the afternoon. Monkeyboy was now amusing himself by throwing carefully rolled balls of dried pigeon poo at everyone. Mama Rat was leaning against one of the caravan's large wooden wheels, behind an old copy of *The Times*. Gigantus was scribbling away once more, pausing every now and then to stare into space and chew his pen, and Sister Moon was throwing metal stars into a wooden pole. She was very good at it, and had just managed to split a fly clean in half.

Sheba sat on an old milking stool, feeling bored. This was hardly the exciting big-city life she had been expecting. Perhaps the days of sitting at the end of Little Pilchton pier hadn't been that dull after all.

'Can I read some of your paper, please, Mama Rat?' she asked. At least now she didn't have to squirrel bits of paper away in Flossy's pen. She smiled when the woman handed her the front page.

The headlines were all about the Great Exhibition. There was a report about a group of seven hundred farmers that had travelled up from the country, a review of the latest exhibits from America and an article moaning about how awful the food was. There were etchings of the most amazing exhibits: the Koh-i-Noor diamond ('the largest in the world!'), the pink crystal fountain ('twenty-seven feet high!') and Mr Faraday's revolutionary electro-magnetic engine ('like captured lightning!'). It seemed as if the exhibition was the only thing the city was talking about, and yet none of the Peculiars had even mentioned it.

'Have any of you been to see the Great Exhibition in the palace of crystal?'

'It's the *Crystal Palace*, dearie,' said Mama Rat. 'And no, we have not as yet had the pleasure.'

'If I even had a spare shilling, I could think of a hundred other things I'd spend it on, rather than go see a load of old tosh in a giant greenhouse,' said Monkeyboy. 'And anyway, they wouldn't let in the likes of us.'

'I don't suppose we'll bother,' said Mama Rat. 'It all sounds very grand, but once you've seen Rome by moon-light, nothing really compares.'

'Well, I'd like to see it,' Sheba said, under her breath.

'Me too,' said Sister Moon. 'We go together sometime.'

Sheba blushed — she'd thought her comment was too quiet to be heard — and then smiled nervously at Sister Moon. *This must be what having a friend is like,* she thought. A proper one, with a single head and no fleece.

She was imaging herself and Moon, strolling through the glass corridors amongst the glorious exhibits, when there was a knock on the yard door.

The Peculiars stared at each other in surprise for a few seconds. Then the more shocking rushed to hide, so as not to frighten off their visitors. Gigantus lumbered into the house, Sheba slid under the old caravan and Monkeyboy crept back to his covered cage.

Sister Moon stood like a palace guard next to Mama Rat, who arranged herself on a bench and called out, 'Please enter!'

The gate swung open slowly and, with much shuffling of feet and backward glances, two figures entered the yard. A woman and a man. From her hiding place, Sheba could see they were barely human – the poorest of the poor. They were wearing little more than rags and were caked to the waist in stinking mud. Their backs were bent, and their shaking limbs were stick-thin. Sheba could see that, underneath a tattered shawl and what might once have been a hat, their eyes were saucer-wide. The mud-stench and pallid skin reminded her of Till, the girl at the show last night.

'Good day,' said Mama Rat, beaming at them from her seat. 'Excuse the messy yard, but it's not often we have company. How can we be helping you?'

There was a flurry of nudging and shoving, until finally the man was pushed forward a step. He removed his hat-like thing and stared studiously at the ground in front of Mama Rat's feet. When he spoke, Sheba was startled to hear a young man's voice. She had been expecting him to be ancient. *What a harsh life these people must lead to age them so*, she thought.

'If you please, your ladyship,' he said. 'We has come to see you, as no other we've asked has the hinclination to give us the time of day. We 'as been all over Sarf London asking for 'elp, and 'as been spat on as often as not. We 'ad all but given up 'ope, until the missus fought of asking yourselves.'

'Help, dearie?' said Mama Rat. 'I think you've got us mistaken. We're just a small sideshow troupe. Unless you want to book us for a performance, we won't be much use to you.'

Sheba could see the pity in her eyes. It mirrored what she herself was feeling. *That's just the way people look at me*, she realised, with a sudden chill. That patronising arch of the eyebrows, the glance that says, 'Poor thing – how miserable it must be to be *her*.' She felt the skin beneath her furry cheeks prickle and blush at having done exactly the thing she most hated to someone else.

'We know that, your ladyness. It's just that we've asked everyone what is supposed to 'elp us – the peelers, the men on the river – and they all just laughed in our face. On account of what we 'eard, we fought this might be the place to come.'

The woman plucked up courage and stepped forward to speak. She too sounded much younger than she looked.

'It's our little girl, ma'am. She came 'ere last night; told us all about you lot and how fantastic and magical you all were and stuff. Then she went out to gather from the river this morning and never come back. All we found is her

– 48 –

picking sack, left on the mud . . . my poor Till . . .' The woman broke down in tears.

From her hiding place beneath the caravan, Sheba gasped. Till!

'Missing, you say?' said Mama Rat. 'And you're sure she hasn't just run away?'

'Run away to what?' asked the man, then looked shocked at his sudden outburst. 'Begging your pardon, your ladyshipness, but you can see from the sight of us that we 'as no better station to run to than the one we got. Picking from the mud is all we is good for. Ain't nowhere for us to run, nor no one what would have us.'

'Hmm, you have a point, dearie,' Mama Rat said. 'Do you have any idea as to what might have happened? Has she failed to come home before?'

'No, your nobleness. Besides skipping off to see you lot last night, she's always done as she was told. Tess thought she might 'ave come back to join you, but I said, "What's so fantastical about a raggedy little mudlark?" Grand folk like you wouldn't want someone like 'er hanging around . . .'

Mama Rat sat and puffed on her pipe for a few moments while the mudlark woman sniffled and the man shuffled his feet.

Sheba reached forwards and clutched the wheel spokes, staring wide-eyed from the shadows. *We have to help find her, we just have to!* She could almost picture Till – lost and lonely somewhere, away from her parents. It was hard enough for Sheba, forever wondering about the family she had never had. Imagine having known that kind of love and having it ripped away from you. *Say we'll help her!* She tried to will the thought across the yard and into Mama Rat's head. If she didn't think it would send Till's ma and da screaming out of the yard, she would have jumped out and begged.

In between the clouds of pipe smoke, Mama Rat caught her eye. Some kind of understanding passed between them.

'I think we might be able to help you, dearies,' she said, slowly.

'You will?' The man looked directly at Mama Rat for the first time, his mouth open in shock. 'You really will?'

'I'm not promising anything,' said Mama Rat. 'As I said, we're just a little sideshow troupe. But we do have some connections and . . . abilities that might be of service, I suppose. And after all, your daughter was a member of our audience, however briefly.'

'Lawd bless ya,' said the man, clapping his hands. From under her spatterings of dirt and grime, the woman beamed with relief. 'And we'll pay you all back some'ow. Even if it takes us fifty years of sifting mud, we will.'

At that moment a large amount of banging and shouting could be heard coming from the upstairs window of the house. Plumpscuttle was stirring.

'Yes, yes, we'll discuss all that later,' said Mama Rat, hurriedly. Sister Moon stepped forward and began ushering the mudpickers towards the gate. 'We'll send word when we have any information for you. Keep your ears open, and please feel free to visit again, should you discover anything yourselves. Good afternoon, dearies!'

''Ang on a minute—' the man began to say, but Sister Moon's firm grip had propelled the pair into the street, slamming the gate behind them.

Moments later, the back door of the house banged open and the bleary and dishevelled form of Plumpscuttle appeared.

'Did I just see some people in my yard?' he bellowed. 'Some strange folk, uninvited on my personal property? Some scrawny street-offal covered in rags and filthy muck?'

'We were just asking them if they knew anyone selling good food,' said Sheba, as she climbed out from under the caravan. 'We were all feeling a little peckish.'

'Peckish? I could eat that scrawny two-headed sheep raw! Get me five helpings of whatever you're having. And make it quick.' He threw a handful of copper pennies out into the yard, then stomped off into the house.

Mama Rat gave Sheba a thoughtful look as Sister Moon scooped up the pennies and headed off to find a street vendor.

'You, young lady, are beginning to prove immensely useful,' she said.

Dinner was a bowl of Penny Dip: fried sheep heart and liver, mixed with onions and dumplings. To Sheba it tasted exotic and delicious, even if the dumplings were slightly gritty. The others shovelled it in their mouths without expression. This was standard fare, as uninspiring for them as fish soup had been for Sheba at Grunchgirdle's.

They ate outside, sitting cross-legged on the yard floor, as Plumpscuttle was occupying the kitchen table. Every now and then the sound of a wet burp echoed through the window.

'So,' said Gigantus. 'What do you make of them mud-grubblers?'

'A bunch of low-life scroungers, if you ask me,' said Monkeyboy. 'Surely we're not going to bother looking for their brat? Probably got munched up by those man-eating monster eels in the river.'

'I recall your start to life wasn't that much higher, half-pint,' said Gigantus, as he licked the last bit of gravy from his spoon.

'That's got nothing to do with it!' Monkeyboy shouted, spraying everyone with a mouthful of half-chewed sheep guts. 'All I'm saying is, what's the point of helping out a load of stinky old mudheads? Don't you know how many people there are in this blooming city? Anyway, it'll only be a few months before they all starve to death whatever we do. If the cholera doesn't get them first.'

'That little girl,' said Sheba, 'happens to be my friend. Her name is Till, and she was very sweet and kind to me. Unlike most people. If there's a way to help her, then I will.'

'Well said, dearie.' Mama Rat gave her a wink. 'Those better off should always try and help the less fortunate. That's why I agreed on behalf of you all. And my little babbies will come in useful, looking for that girl.'

'In what way?' Sheba couldn't think how a miniature circus would be any help in finding a missing mudlark.

'Oh, my boys are very good at detecting things. They can go from one end of this city to the other without anyone so much as catching a whiff of them. They've found all sorts of bits and pieces for me over the years. All sorts indeed.'

Sheba wanted to ask more, but a deep voice boomed out from the kitchen.

'When you disgusting bunch of aberrations have finished stuffing your fat faces, there's work to be done! Get off your lazy arses, and get this place ready for a show!'

Chapter Six

IN WHICH THE PECULIARS TRY SNIFFING BY
THE RIVER (FOR CLUES, THAT IS).

Early morning on Bermondsey waterfront, and the tanneries were already pumping streams of thick red fluid into the Thames. A mixture of chemicals, acid and waste, it let out fumes that could take your eyebrows off at fifty paces. At the tannery doors, a steady stream of pure-pickers had begun to gather. The leather works needed excrement for tanning the hides and each carried a bucket of fresh dog droppings that they had collected from the streets the day before. Boats had begun to row, sail and steam up the river. And waiting for the tide to ebb were packs of tattered children. Mudlarks, just like Till.

Sheba tugged her hood over her head, hiding her face in its shadows. Her delicate nose was completely swamped by the disgusting aromas. It stank, it was freezing, and she was bored beyond measure. They had been out here since dawn, although it seemed like months of her life had passed by, standing on these muck-spattered cobbles.

When they had first made their way through the morning crowd, she had marvelled at the huge amount of people. More than the audiences at Plumpscuttle's shows. More than the people milling outside her window on Brick Lane. She had kept close to Gigantus, one little furry hand clutching the back of his jumper, as he steamed through the throngs like an icebreaker. Then it had seemed marvellous and exhilarating to be out and about in the big city at last, but the novelty had soon worn off.

They had been asking questions of folk on the waterfront for hours. Or rather, Gigantus had been asking questions while the others lurked in the background. Their peculiarities didn't exactly encourage people to speak to them. They were usually too busy staring to even hear the question.

Gigantus, on the other hand, used his huge size to great effect. When he stepped in front of someone it was like being confronted by a small mountain. People stood trembling while he asked about the missing mudlark, then told him every scrap of information they thought could be of any possible value, and very often more besides. He was currently towering over a shivering bargeman who was babbling about some spoons that were hidden under his bedroom floorboards.

Sheba felt useless. She had thought she might be able to sniff something out with her nose, a hint of Till's scent perhaps, but all she could smell were the tanneries and the stinking river. She had also imagined that a missing girl would be big news amongst the people of the riverside. It was becoming obvious that none of them gave a monkey's.

Beneath all the boats and steamers, beneath the oozing brown water and the floating lumps of stuff that swirled in it, was the mud that Till had spent her life combing for dubious treasure. In her cape pocket, Sheba ran her fingers over the cracked green marble. *Is she down there now?* she wondered. *Did she get sucked under the cold, clammy mud? Or did someone take her from the river to a different place entirely?*

They were upsetting thoughts, but Sheba couldn't help them. Monkeyboy was right: in a city teeming with so many people, what were the chances of finding one insignificant little girl?

Thinking like that won't help. She decided to concentrate on something else entirely. From deep within her hood, she focused on the river traffic. A splendid three-masted clipper was gliding its way down to the Pool of London, making the tiny skiffs and wherries around it look like ants. Something about its majestic lines and jutting prow stirred a feeling in Sheba, but it was so vague and distant she didn't know what it was, or what it meant. An early memory, perhaps, but fluttering just beyond her reach: another loose thread. It was as if her mind was trying to send her a message about a life she had had before her earliest of memories. Had she ever been on a ship?

Had she ever lived in a white house with a marble floor? Probably not. It was more likely that she was dumped at the doorstep of the workhouse by some poor wretch of a woman, like Till's ma. A starving pauper struck dumb with horror at the hairy child she had given birth to.

Just the thought of it made Sheba's head swim with overpowering emotions. Anger at being abandoned, shame at being so unnatural and hideous, sorrow for whoever had been desperate enough to abandon their own child. Old feelings that were best left deep inside her head. She banished them there now, turning her eyes away from the clipper.

Gigantus finished talking to the bargeman, leaving him to scurry away into the mist, and then stomped over. He looked frustrated.

'Another petty criminal who doesn't actually know anything,' he said. 'If we were looking for stolen silver-ware we'd have solved this case twenty times over by now.'

Beside Sheba, Monkeyboy peeped out from under his battered top hat. 'Letting that lumpy brute ask all the questions isn't getting us anywhere,' he said.

'I suppose you have a better idea?' Gigantus replied through gritted teeth.

'I have, as it happens. Didn't Mama Rat used to know some bloke down on the docks? Fat Albert, or something? Why don't we go and ask him?'

'You might be on to something there, Monkey,' said Mama Rat, thoughtfully. 'It was Large 'Arry I used to be acquainted with. I remember he still owes me a favour or two.'

'What are we waiting for, then?' Monkeyboy said.

'Nice to see you take interest, Monkey.' Sister Moon patted the top of his hat.

Monkeyboy shrugged it off with a pout. 'Yes, well. Anything's better than standing around here any longer, isn't it?'

Sheba couldn't help but agree.

Sheba had thought the roads and bridges of the city crowded, but they were nothing compared to the chaos of the wharves.

Piles of lopsided wooden warehouses leant against each other, stretching out into the river on rickety wooden stakes. Boats of every shape and size were crammed so tightly against each other, it seemed as though the smaller ones would burst into clouds of matchsticks at any second. A scribbly mess of ships' masts and wooden cranes blocked the sky, and rope was everywhere in twists and loops, tying everything together like a giant spider's web. And in between it all were hordes of bustling, shouting people. They were loading and unloading ships, hauling crates and boxes in and out of warehouses, on and off carts and barrows. It made Sheba dizzy just to watch them.

The Peculiars scuttled along the dockside, dodging swinging bales of cotton and sweaty rivermen, and all the time following Mama Rat and her cloud of pipe smoke. She didn't stop until she came to a huge wooden warehouse with the words 'Pickle Herring Wharf' emblazoned across the front. There she stood for a few minutes, scanning the faces of the scurrying dockmen. Just when Sheba was beginning to think they were looking in the wrong place, Mama Rat clapped her hands together and laughed. She walked briskly over to a stack of crates and coiled rope, where a man was sitting, whittling away at a hunk of wood with a pocket knife.

He looked up, and for a moment his brows raised in surprise. He quickly pulled them back into a frown, but not before getting a good look at the rest of the Peculiars.

'You 'ave fallen in with a strange lot,' he said.

'Nothing wrong with being a bit strange, dearie,' said Mama Rat. 'Everyone, meet Large 'Arry. A very old friend of mine.'

'Friends, is it?' said 'Arry. 'I 'aven't seen hide nor hair of you for years. I've got customers in Mozambique what are better friends than you.'

'Now, now, 'Arry.' Mama Rat looked hurt. 'Don't be like that.'

Sheba stared at the man from beneath her hood. He

certainly was large, although not compared to the huge bulk of Gigantus. Most of 'Arry's size was around his belly, which strained to burst out of his woollen jumper. He had shaggy grey hair and a grizzly beard, turned yellow around his mouth from tobacco smoke. He looked just how she'd imagine an old sea captain to be. He carved off a few more slivers of wood, before Mama Rat's exaggerated pout made him mellow.

'All right, then,' he said. 'What is it brings you and your misshapen crew down on the docks? After something, I don't doubt.'

'Just some information,' said Mama Rat. 'About a mudlark girl who's gone missing from the river.'

'One of those poor scraps what go rooting about in the filthy mud between the jetties, you mean? I 'aven't heard nothing about that, but then . . .' He paused. 'What's this information worth, exactly?'

'It's worth you keeping your face the right shape,' said Gigantus, knuckles cracking. He appeared to be tired of waiting.

'Stop that, Gigantus,' said Mama Rat. 'I told you, 'Arry's an old friend. There's no need to scare him.'

'And I been threatened by worse than the likes of you,' 'Arry added. Even so, his hands seemed to shake a little as he went back to his whittling.

'*Please*, Mr Large,' Sheba said. She didn't want to draw attention to herself, but she was desperate to find out what he knew. 'The girl that's missing is my friend. I *have* to find out what happened to her. Anything you tell us will help, I'm certain.'

'Arry looked up from his piece of wood, into Sheba's pleading amber eyes. If he noticed the fur on her face, he didn't show it. The frown lines on his brow softened.

'I 'ad a daughter meself, once,' he said. 'About your age. She went missing too. Fell off a jetty and drowned.' He sighed and tucked his knife away. 'There was something a few days ago. Not about a girl, but still . . . I was unloading down on St Saviour's dock, when some of the lads started talking rubbish about noises in the fog and children going missing at low tide. Now, I don't hold with all that talk about monsters in the river and suchlike, but I do believe that there was some of them mudlarks what went out and never came back. As far as I heard, anyway.'

'What do you think happened to them?' asked Sheba.

Large 'Arry shrugged. 'What do *you* think? Sucked down in the mud, I should expect. Who would be so stupid as to go walking around out there? And if the clay didn't get them, there's plenty of other things that might. This city's full of evil, you know. Murderers, thieves, baby farmers chucking kiddies in the river, doctors chopping up grave-robbed bodies . . . things you wouldn't believe. London ain't no kind of a place to be growing up in. Not if you're skint paupers like you lot.'

The old sailor pulled his knife out again and went back to his whittling, signifying the meeting was over. Mama Rat thanked him, and he grunted in a way that might be perceived as affectionate.

The Peculiars began to make their way back through the maze of docks to London Bridge.

Other children are missing too. The thought rolled around in Sheba's head like a marble. If that were true, then what had they stumbled into? And where could Till be now?

She was so wrapped up in her thoughts that she didn't notice the shape of a dark figure in the shadow of a warehouse doorway. The light was dim there, dusky enough to hide the long tendrils of matted hair beneath a large hat, the straggly beard, and the strangely curved sword that hung underneath a long coat. It even hid the thick lines of black paint that spread from one side of his face to the other, but not the gleam of his eyes as he watched the Peculiars make their way home.

Chapter Seven

At the show that night, Sheba half expected to see Till, back to tell her she had run away from her life as a mudlark for something better and less stinky. But there was no sign. And worrying about her made it hard for Sheba to put on a proper performance.

'You'd better start making an effort,' Plumpscuttle had warned her afterwards, 'or it's back to that dump at the seaside for you, missy.'

Now she had something else to worry about.

The next morning she lay in bed long after the others

had arisen, staring miserably at the patches of damp, cracked plaster on the ceiling.

This isn't helping, she finally said to herself. *I'm going to get up and try twice as hard to find Till today.*

In one determined movement, she sat up and threw back her tattered blanket. She was just about to pull on her pinafore and go downstairs, when she noticed a large, rectangular lump in Gigantus's giant mattress. She recalled the way the big man was always scribbling away in his journal. Was it a secret diary, maybe? Or a manual on how to smash someone into a pulp?

The voice in her head told her to leave it well alone. It was a bad idea to pry into anyone's secret books, but if you did it to a strongman over two metres tall, you were asking for trouble. The kind of trouble that required stitches afterwards.

But she just couldn't help herself. The book-shaped bump seemed to cry out to her. Her fingertips itched at the thought of uncovering it. *Maybe just a tiny peek,* she thought, as she reached under the bedding . . .

It was indeed a book. A large, leather-bound one, much bigger than his journal. She picked it up and opened the heavy cover. On the first page, written in careful copper-plate script, was '*The Thrilling Escapades of Agnes Throbbington* by Gertrude Lacygusset'.

Agnes Throbbington? Gertrude Lacygusset? Sheba opened the first page, listening all the while for footsteps on the stairs.

Agnes could feel her tiny heart flutter away like a tiny fluttery thing.

Across the crowded ballroom stood Jeremy Gristle, the local pig doctor and the champion of her dreams.

He looked out across the dance floor with his manly steel-grey eyes. His face was elegantly chiselled, with a firm, manly jaw. His raven hair hung about his broad, manly shoulders. He wore a silk topcoat and a waistcoat embroidered with silver flowers. That was quite manly, too.

All around Jeremy farmers' daughters and rural spinsters were draped in flouncy layers of every colour, but he cared not a fig for them. Ever since their eyes had met over the pigsty three days ago, Agnes knew all he could think about was her. Thank goodness her father's prize porker had developed chronic diarrhoea or they might never have met.

When Jeremy caught her eye, Agnes's breath stuck in her throat. Even from across the ballroom, it felt as though she was falling deep into his gaze, as if their very souls were bleeding into one great big squishy blob of true love. She twitched her nose in as pig-like a manner as possible, and gave a little oink of delight . . .

Sheba heard a creak from the stair floorboards. Her heart pounding in her chest, she shoved the book back under the mattress and tried to look as though she was just getting up from her bed. After a few seconds, when Gigantus failed to burst into the room, she got up and peeked down the stairs. They were completely empty.

Serves you right for being so nosey, she thought. But she couldn't help feeling slightly disturbed as she padded down the narrow stairs to find the others.

They were in the yard, debating what course of action to take next.

'Maybe we go back to docks,' Sister Moon was saying. 'Ask more questions.'

'What's the point in that?' Gigantus paused in his exercises. Today he was lifting the wooden caravan up and down off the ground. 'Nobody really knows anything. We'll just hear more claptrap about monsters eating children in the fog. Morning, Sheba.'

Sheba looked at Gigantus with new eyes. Was he really Gertrude Lacygusset, romantic novelist? She tried to cover up her confusion by joining in the debate. 'But if others *have* been taken,' she said, 'then couldn't it all be connected?'

'Why would anyone want to kidnap a bunch of starving river rats?' Monkeyboy was perched on the privy roof, nibbling his toenails. 'If you're going to nab children, you'd be best off taking ones that aren't going to pop their clogs in a month or two.'

'On the contrary,' said Mama Rat. 'If you were taking children, then the lowest of the low is where you'd start. After all, apart from us, who's even noticed they're gone?'

'Maybe one of them doctors has taken them to peel open and look inside. Or something worse. I heard a story once about a butcher who chopped up people and made them into pies. Maybe he's decided to make Mudlark Muffins instead.'

'That's my friend you're talking about, Monkeyboy!' Sheba snapped, and was surprised to see him look ashamed.

The argument was interrupted by a fluttering and flapping of wings as something that almost resembled a bird dropped out of the sky and onto the fence. It sat there, blinking and attempting to coo.

'What is that?' said Monkeyboy, his eyes nearly popping out of his head.

'I think it a pigeon,' Sister Moon said.

It did have a beak, and some tatty things that might be feathers, but it didn't look much like a bird to Sheba. Not unless it was some new, London variety that had been crossed with a rat and nested at the bottom of a coal scuttle.

'Urgh, I flipping hate pigeons,' Monkeyboy clapped his hands and tried to scare it away. 'Rats with wings, that's what they are!'

'Just be careful what you're saying about rats,' said Mama Rat.

'You leave that bird alone!' Gigantus stomped over from the caravan and plucked the pigeon from the fence with one hand. Sheba thought he might crush the little thing like an eggshell, but instead he held it tenderly between his huge fingers as he carefully removed a piece of paper from its leg.

'I wouldn't touch that if I were you,' said Monkeyboy, looking disgusted. 'You'll catch something horrid.'

'What are you doing?' Sheba asked.

'It's a letter from an old acquaintance of mine,' Gigantus replied. 'Sent by homing pigeon. I gave him this bird years ago. Never thought he'd actually use it.'

'Sneepsnood?' Mama Rat asked, and Gigantus nodded.

'He wants to see us today. Says it's urgent.'

Sheba noticed a wary glance pass between the two.

Sister Moon also seemed to tense beside her.

'Who's Sneepsnood?' Sheba whispered.

'Man that Gigantus know. I only see him one time, but not trust him. Criminal, I think.'

'Well, we'd best oblige him then,' said Mama Rat.

Sneepsnood's Reconstituted Metal Goods Emporium was a tiny shop on Whitechapel High Street. The mullioned windows that faced the road were covered in grime. If you peered really closely, you could just about make out display shelves crammed with metal goods of all descriptions. There were old music boxes, keys of every size and shape, tin cans stuffed with rusty nails, kettles, buckets, scissors, shears, knives, forks and bits of machinery that had fallen off various steamers and ended up in the river. None of it looked particularly appealing, but then it wasn't supposed to.

There was a tiny, muck-spattered sign hanging over the door, and when the Peculiars entered, a bell gave a dismal tinkle. The inside of the shop was just as cluttered as the window display. A range of dressers and tables, most with missing legs propped up by books and old bricks, filled all but the tiniest bit of floor space. Every shelf and surface was covered with more useless metal items, some of which had entirely dissolved into little piles of rust. There was a thick coating of dust over everything, broken only by the tiny trails of hundreds of mouse footprints.

At the sound of the bell, a man shuffled out from the back of the shop. He was extraordinarily lanky and wore a tight, threadbare suit. He looked like a cloth-wrapped beanpole. His thinning grey hair was plastered back from his scalp with lashings of pomade, and a pair of wire spectacles perched on the end of his hooked nose.

'Ah, you got my message then,' he said.

'Good to see you again, Jeremiah,' said Gigantus. He carefully handed over the pigeon, which he had carried in a gentle cradle of his huge fingers all the way from Brick Lane. Sneepsnood grabbed it as if it were an old feather duster and rammed it, squawking, into a nearby cage. Gigantus's craggy face scowled. *I really am learning lots about him today*, thought Sheba, as she looked on from beneath her hood.

'Come round the back,' said Sneepsnood, oblivious to how close he had just come to a pummelling. 'I think there's room.'

The Peculiars followed him through a door at the rear, and there was a series of clatters as Gigantus dragged half the shop along with him. After much squeezing and manoeuvring, they stepped through into the back room.

It was almost as cluttered as the shop, but instead of metal junk, it was full of silverware. Spoons, ladles, bowls, plates, goblets and tureens; stacks of them on tables and benches all around the room. A big hearth filled one wall, and a fire was roaring inside. A blackened crucible sat in the middle, tended by a scruffy little boy. Every now and then he fed another piece of silver into the pot and watched it slowly dissolve into the thick, glinting soup of molten metal. On the workbench next to him were piled twenty or more bars of solid silver. Sheba realised what Sister Moon meant about the man being a criminal.

'Now,' said Sneepsnood, turning to face them with a knowing smirk. 'Word comes to me you've been looking for someone down on the waterfront.'

Mama Rat raised an eyebrow. 'Word travels fast, Jeremiah. How did you get to hear of that?'

'There aren't many . . . ahem . . . *groups* like yours in the city.' Sneepsnood smiled, showing grey gums and yellow teeth. 'And you seem to have asked an awful lot of people. Caused quite a stir in the underworld, believe me. Folk thought the peelers had started some new kind of task-force or something.'

'Well, it's nothing to do with the law,' said Gigantus. 'We're just trying to find a missing girl, that's all.'

'I'm sure you are, I'm sure you are!' Sneepsnood flapped his gangly hands and smiled even wider. 'Very honourable too, I must say. Most public-spirited of you.'

'But what has this got to do with you?' Mama Rat asked. Sheba could see she didn't trust the man.

'Well, nothing at first,' said Sneepsnood. 'Just an interesting snippet, I thought. Nice to know what my old friends are up to.' He gave another of his unsettling smiles. 'But then, as you know, I have a range of *clients*, from all walks of life.'

'I know that very well, Jeremiah,' said Gigantus.

'Well, it so happens that one of my patrons, a very well-to-do lady who has sadly lost her own son, had already asked me to keep an ear out for this kind of thing.'

'So you told her all about us,' said Gigantus. His voice was a few shades short of a growl.

'Well . . .' said Sneepsnood, 'I may have mentioned it. But only to help further your enquiries, of course.'

'Of course.'

'Anyway, this lady would like to meet with you, and asked if I would request your presence at Christ Church graveyard this very afternoon. At one o'clock, if you please.'

'Why the graveyard?' Sheba asked. In her curiosity she had forgotten herself, and now found she had drawn the unwelcome attention of Sneepsnood. His gaze was like being slowly covered in grease, and it was all she could do to meet his eyes without shuddering.

'A mutually convenient public place of easily recognisable location,' he said, in one long sneer. 'Suggested it myself, in fact.'

'Very well,' said Mama Rat. 'We shall consider it. Thank you for passing on the message.'

'My deep and abiding pleasure,' said Sneepsnood. The man fawned and smiled a bit more as they left the tiny shop, and even followed them out into the street to wave goodbye. The Peculiars waited until they were well out of his sight before pausing beside a coffee seller to discuss what had happened.

'Thank crikey we're out of there,' said Monkeyboy. 'I was about to be sick. That bloke has more slime than a bucketful of slugs.'

'Well,' said Mama Rat. 'That was all a bit bizarre.'

'I know he and I go way back,' said Gigantus, 'but I can't deny he's trouble.'

'What we do about lady?' said Sister Moon.

There was much rubbing of chins, fur and tails before Sheba found the courage to speak up.

'I think we should go,' she said. 'After all, there's not much else we can do, and if it helps us find Till . . .'

'You're right,' said Mama Rat. 'But maybe not all of us. We don't want to give the poor woman nightmares.'

'You and Sheba go,' said Sister Moon. 'You know what to ask, and Sheba might sniff something. She very clever at that.'

Underneath her fur, Sheba blushed. Another compliment. What was the world coming to?

'Very well,' said Gigantus. 'But the rest of us will be nearby. Just in case.'

Christ Church was literally around the corner from Brick Lane. Made from grimy white stone, with a three-tiered tower at the front, it was easily recognisable for miles around. Crumbling hovels clustered around it, almost as if they themselves were bowing down to worship.

'Fascinating places, churchyards, don't you think?' Mama Rat said as she and Sheba walked round to the graveyard at the back. 'Until they built the new cemeteries, there was barely any room here for all the dead. The gravediggers used to have to chop their way down through all the arms and legs to fit the new ones in. There must be thousands and thousands of corpses under our feet right now.'

Sheba shivered. She had expected it to be difficult to spot the lady, but she was the only person present, seated upon a stone bench amongst the mass of crooked gravestones. From a distance, it looked as though she was hidden in shadow, but as Sheba walked closer, she could see it was how she was dressed.

She wore very fine clothing, but every last stitch was black. Her skirts were thick velvet, her bodice embroidered with the shadows of twining flowers. A shawl hung over her shoulders, a bonnet covered her pinned-up hair, and a lace veil hid her face. She looked like an absence of light and colour, as if something had come along and snipped a woman-shaped hole out of the world. The only bits of her skin visible were the tips of her white fingers where they poked from the end of her black lace gloves.

As Mama Rat and Sheba wove their way through the gravestones, the lace veil twitched, then moved as the woman turned her head. Sheba found it unnerving to be watched without being able to see any eyes. *Although*, she thought, *a veil would be a good way to hide your face. If I had one, I could go anywhere, and no one would know I was at all different.*

'Good day,' said Mama Rat, as they reached the bench.

'Good day,' said the woman.

Sheba wondered if she should say 'good day' too, but generally children were expected to be silent unless spoken to. Instead she took a subtle sniff.

Besides the smell of the graveyard itself, and the stench

of horse manure and rubbish from the road beyond, Sheba picked up a rather cold and sharp smell around the woman – with a trace of something else, a sweet aroma that, for once, she couldn't place. She frowned.

'Please, do have a seat,' said the woman, breaking Sheba's thread of concentration.

Mama Rat sat beside her on the bench, leaving Sheba room to hop on the end.

'I take it you're the lady that Mr Sneepsnood has been representing,' she said.

'Indeed,' said the woman. 'My name is Mrs Crowley.' She spoke with a strange lisp. 'I understand you have been making enquiries about lost children?'

'May I ask what interest our enquiries are to you?' asked Mama Rat.

There was a long pause, as if the woman were reluctant to speak. Finally, she gave a soft sigh and said, 'I too am searching for a lost child. My son went missing some months ago. He was playing by the shoreline one morning and never returned. Which is why I contacted Mr Sneepsnood. And several other businessmen up and down the river besides. I thought they might have some news.'

'Surely you'd be better off speaking to the peel . . . I mean the police?' Mama Rat said.

'Oh, I have tried,' Mrs Crowley replied. 'And they have assured me repeatedly they are 'looking into it'. But I thought . . . if I knew someone else in the same position, we could somehow join forces. Share notes. And to know someone else who felt as I do . . . it would help me immeasurably.'

'It's clear you fear the worst, if you've gone into mourning already.' Mama Rat gestured with her pipe at the black dress.

'Oh yes, the veil,' said Mrs Crowley. 'I know it might be premature, that there still could be hope. But without my little boy . . . it wouldn't feel right to go about dressed as normal. I'm sure you understand.'

Mama Rat lit a fresh pipe. 'We'd like to help, of course, but we've only just started looking into the matter ourselves.'

'I see. And is it your daughter that has gone missing? Or a son like mine perhaps?'

'Neither,' said Mama Rat. 'Never had any children myself. Oh, besides Sheba here, of course. No, we're looking into the matter on behalf of some friends.'

'Sheba . . .' For the first time, the veil turned towards her, and for an instant Sheba thought she saw the glint of an eye shining through the thick lace veil.

'Good day,' she said, rather belatedly.

The veil didn't move for several seconds, as if the lady was examining Sheba closely, then it turned back to Mama Rat. 'May I ask who those friends are?'

'I'm afraid that's confidential,' said Mama Rat.

'I understand,' said Mrs Crowley. 'But perhaps you could let me know of anything you might discover?'

'Of course,' said Mama Rat.

'That would be wonderful.' Mrs Crowley clasped her hands as if satisfied, although without seeing her face it was hard to tell. Almost as an afterthought, she took a calling card from her pocket. She moved to give it to Mama Rat, then at the last moment reached past her and presented it to Sheba. 'I look forward to hearing some news. Soon, I hope.'

Sheba looked down at the embossed piece of pasteboard, printed with expensive copperplate font. 'Mrs N. Crowley, 17 Paradise Street, Bermondsey', it read.

With a nod of her shrouded head, the veiled lady rose and left the churchyard.

Sheba and Mama Rat stared after her.

'Well,' Mama Rat said eventually. 'It's not often you meet someone stranger than us in this city.'

Before Sheba could reply, Gigantus, Sister Moon and Monkeyboy came dashing around the corner of the church. They looked visibly relieved when they saw the others sitting on the bench, and slowed their pace through the maze of headstones.

'Thank goodness you all right,' said Sister Moon, panting for breath. 'We saw strange man follow you. Long coat and big hat. We could not see face.'

'Where?' Sheba said, looking around the churchyard. 'We didn't see anyone.'

'He was walking right behind you,' said Monkeyboy. 'I'm surprised you didn't smell him with that weird nose of yours.'

Sheba was surprised too. 'Probably just a passer-by,' she said, but she felt annoyed with herself. Had she missed something?

'What did you find out?' Gigantus asked. All three of them were clearly itching to know.

'We'll tell you back at the house,' said Mama Rat, with an ominous look around her. 'Away from prying eyes and ears.'

Chapter Eight

IN WHICH ANOTHER MUDLARK
IS ALMOST MUNCHED.

Barnabus Bilge awoke to the nearby bells of St Mary's striking three in the morning. The chimes had woken him at exactly the same time every day since his very first memory. *Years and years of getting up in the middle of the night and I still hate it,* he thought, as he wriggled out of the bed he shared with his mother, father and three other children. He stepped over a few more kids sleeping on the floor, and went through into the kitchen.

He didn't have time to light a fire to make breakfast; his mother would do that in an hour's time when she got his sisters up for work. Instead there was a bucket of pump water on the table. He took a scoop and slurped some, then splashed the rest over his face to wake himself up. It was a lurid brown colour and tasted rancid, but at least it didn't have anything disgusting floating in it today.

He peered at the piece of cracked mirror standing on the mantelpiece and saw a grubby teenager with eyes that looked much too old for his face. He rubbed at the fluff on his cheeks, wondering when it would ever turn to whiskers so he could grow a nice pair of sideburns.

There was a pot of cold gruel hanging over the fire, left over from last night's dinner. Judging by the little footprints all over the cauldron, the mice had been at it again. At least they'd left a bit for breakfast. He swallowed a couple of gloopy spoonfuls, and then headed out.

The fog was thick again this morning. Out on the banks, the mudlarks were back. Even tales of missing children and river monsters couldn't keep them away, for they had no choice. Pick from the mud, or starve. If the Thames had been full of piranha fish they would still have been there, trying to snatch as much as they could before their legs were chewed through.

Barney prided himself on being the best picker on the south banks. He was slightly less scrawny than the rest, thanks to his success, and the others paused to give him respectful glances as he passed. He clutched a pole twice as tall as himself, and it was this that gave him his edge.

Whilst the other mudlarks had nothing but their own bare feet with which to test for sinkholes and broken glass, Barney Bilge used his pole. He poked it systematically as he slurped through the thigh-deep slop, finding solid footings that could take him out further than any of the others. Every now and then he'd strike something under the surface that he could scoop out, too. He'd found such treasures as a crate of pickled eggs, a silver plate and four human skulls. By mudlark standards, he was a millionaire.

Low tide had come early today, and Barney was pleased he wouldn't have to waste time waiting for it. Instead, he waded straight in, trying not to shiver as his bare toes slid into the chilled jelly of the mud.

Dip, dip, dip went his pole, as if he was some peculiar wading bird. Every now and then he stopped, fished something out and tucked it in his sack. It wasn't long before he had a pipe, half a pair of spectacles and a leather boot sole.

The fog folded around him. Step, prod, step, prod. His mind was just beginning to wander into a daydream about being king of England when his pole struck something solid.

He snapped back to reality, and with a hunter's zeal, thumped his pole down again. It struck a second time, with a metallic clang. There was definitely something down there, and it was big.

In a move he very soon came to regret, he began shifting his pole forward, bringing it down hard again and again. Thunk! Thunk! Thunk! The thing was directly underneath him, and seemed to be around three metres long. He wormed one of his feet further into the mud to get a feel, and soon met a smooth surface, studded here and there with spikes or bolts. His little toes followed the contours, wondering what on earth it could be. There seemed to be several hard layers, or plates, on top of one another, which meant it probably wasn't a chest or crate. Almost at the end, he felt a length of pipe or tubing, and then . . . it *moved* . . .

Barney froze as the movement came again. The thing had juddered beneath his foot. He quickly looked around to see if any other mudlarks were nearby in case he needed help. That was when he noticed the bright-red tentacles, poking up from the mud all around him.

At first he thought they might be a bizarre family of eels, but then he noticed a puff of steam escape from the end of one, then another. Soon all of them were gushing hot smoke, just as the thing beneath him began to grind its way upwards more violently.

One of the things that had kept Barney alive so long on the river was that he was *fast*. Several times he had felt the mud try to suck him under, and he had managed to pull his feet free and scrabble his way out of danger. Now, his reflexes kicked in again, and he flung himself off the back of whatever-it-was and began pelting his way back to shore.

Anyone who has ever tried to run through deep mud will tell you it is virtually impossible. The quicker Barney tried to pull his feet out, the harder the river bed sucked them back in. He soon fell on all fours, and began a frantic scrambling that was part crawling, part swimming.

As he wriggled his way to the bank, panting and choking, with fat gobbets of stinking mud flying into his face and mouth, he heard a great roar from behind him. Something had exploded out of the mud, and was thrashing about on the surface. Barney could hear the clank and grind of metal, the hiss and chuff of a steam engine. When he chanced a quick look over his shoulder, he saw a huge, crab-like beast with a glowing yellow eye. Its tentacles poured smoke out into the foggy air, and two jagged claws waved about, snipping and snapping as they tried to grab his feet. In the glare from its huge eyeball, Barney spotted a movement: a shadow of something inside the beast itself. A bearded face, painted all over with black lines and swirls, floating in the centre of the eye like a diseased iris.

With a scream of terror, Barney doubled his efforts, slithering through the mud like a demented eel. Luckily for him, some of the other mudlarks saw him thrashing around, and dashed to grab his hands. Just as the monster's claws clanged shut on what would have been his ankle, Barney was hauled out of the mud and on to the riverbank, where he lay panting and crying at the same time. The mudlarks looked out at the river, faces pale beneath the muck and dirt, as the fog closed in around the clawed creature, and it slowly vanished from sight.

Chapter Nine

IN WHICH MONKEYBOY HAS A DISAGREEMENT
WITH A GIANT OCTOPUS.

The rendezvous with Mrs Crowley was still on Sheba's mind the next morning. Something about it was bothering her as she sipped her coffee in the kitchen. To take her mind off it, she picked up Mama Rat's newspaper once more and found herself looking at the small advertisement section. Her breath caught for a moment.

On these pages there were usually offers of miracle cures – for baldness or flatulence – and requests for new maids and governesses, but she had once seen a notice placed by a mother searching for her child. It hadn't been a heart-wrenching plea, or a dramatic tale of loss, just a simple 'Mother searching for daughter given up when three. Blonde hair, blue eyes, answered to Kitty.' Ever since then she had read the advertisement section with a mixture of longing and loathing. What if she's looking for you, too? the voice in her head would say. There could be a notice about you in this very paper. She detested that voice, and the way a part of her believed it. Just throw the paper away this time, she told herself. Don't even bother reading it. So she did.

Out in the yard, Gigantus was limbering up for his morning's exercises. Sister Moon sat with her eyes closed, deep in thought. Mama Rat had a saucepan of hot, soapy water, and was trying to coax her rats out of a hole by the kitchen door.

'You're not seriously going to give those wretched rodents a bath, are you?' Monkeyboy called down from his perch on the fence.

'I am indeed,' said Mama Rat, over her shoulder. 'And if you make any of your stupid jokes, you'll be next.'

'Not likely. I've spent years building up this unique aroma, you know.' The threat of clean water made him skip neatly along the fence, a safe distance away, before he gave a sudden yell. 'Visitors again! It's them mudlark folk back, and they've brought someone with them.'

Everyone except Mama Rat and Sister Moon dashed back into the house. Sheba shut the back door behind her, then turned to peer through the keyhole.

There came a weak tapping at the gate, before it swung

open to reveal once more the cowering forms of Till's parents. They looked more than ever like two lumps of mud that had somehow grown legs. Between them stood another mudlark, this one literally caked in drying clay and stinking like an open sewer. For a moment Sheba's heart leapt, thinking it might be Till, but on closer inspection she could see it was a boy. He clutched the splintered end of a long pole in one hand.

'Begging your gentlefolk's pardon, but we 'as some information which we fink might be of use,' said the man, bobbing his head like a very humble woodpecker. 'You did say we was to call on you if that should be the case . . .'

'Of course, of course,' said Mama Rat. 'Come in, please.'

The three of them shuffled into the yard and shut the gate behind them. When they were safely inside, and with no means of immediate escape, Mama Rat beckoned to the other Peculiars in the house.

'If you don't mind,' she said, 'I'd like my colleagues to hear this. They do look slightly unusual, but please don't be alarmed.'

The mudlarks stared as Sheba, Monkeyboy and Gigantus came out of the kitchen and into the yard.

'We is . . . er . . . very honoured to make your acquaintance,' said the father mudlark at last, taking off his hat and holding it on his chest. Sheba felt a surge of grateful admiration. Many other folk would have run screaming, or at least fainted with shock.

'Pleased to meet you, too,' said Sheba.

The mud-caked boy goggled at her, but the lady managed a kind of smile.

'What you have to tell us?' asked Sister Moon. The mudlarks looked briefly startled, as they remembered why they had come to this surreal freak show in the first place.

'If you please, your unusual-nesses, our friend Barney 'ere 'as an interesting tale to tell you. Only this very morning, 'e was nearly snaffled by a creature from under the mud.' The man nudged Barney with his elbow, dislodging several clumps of stinking muck from the boy's clothes. 'Go on, son, tell the ladies and gentlemen what 'appened.'

Barney blinked a few times, then opened his mouth to speak, making little cracks in the layer of dried mud that coated his face. He told them about the crab-thing and how it had come out of the mud to try and grab him, about his escape and how he had been almost dragged to Brick Lane as soon as the other mudlarks heard his story.

There was a long silence afterwards, as everyone considered his bizarre tale.

'This thing that tried to get you,' asked Sheba, 'do you think it could have been a machine?'

'A machine, miss?' Barney stared at her as if she was mad, as well as very hairy. 'T'weren't no machine. It was a monster. A giant, hissing crab, just like I told you. And there was an eye. A yellow eye, with a 'orrible face in it. It must have been some kind of demon, like what the street preachers go on about.'

'But it had pipes and steam. Monsters aren't driven by engines.'

'Leave it, Sheba,' said Monkeyboy. 'I think he's drunk too much river mud. It's probably melted his brain.'

'Be quiet, you little gremlin,' said Gigantus, 'or I'll melt your brain. Pull it right out of your ears and fry it over the stove.'

'Do you think this thing is what took our little'uns?' asked the woman. 'You don't think it's eaten them, do you? I can't bear to think it: my little Till gobbled up by a giant crab . . .'

'It can't have eaten them, on account of it being a *machine*, you stup— erk!' Monkeyboy was cut off in mid-insult as Gigantus's huge hand clamped his mouth.

'I think it may well be the thing that took the children,' said Mama Rat. 'And I'm sure they haven't been eaten. We'll continue our search and let you know as soon as we find anything. Perhaps you'd better leave before our tailed friend here says something truly offensive.'

With even more bowing and scraping, the mudlarks backed out of the yard, just as the sound of the front door slamming signalled Plumpscuttle's return.

'Shut the gate, shut the gate!' hissed Mama Rat, but it was too late.

Plumpscuttle's head appeared at the kitchen window in time to see the last mudlark disappear.

'What's this?' he yelled. 'What's this?'

'Here we go,' Gigantus muttered.

They all turned sheepishly to face the house as Plumpscuttle wobbled down the kitchen steps, his face growing steadily more purple.

'People in my yard again? Uninvited trespassers on my property? You bunch of walking monsters know that visitors are forbidden here, don't you? If people want to gawp at you, then I expect them to pay me for the privilige!'

He must have had a pie that didn't agree with him, thought Sheba. *And now he wants to take it out on the rest of us.*

'Now, now—' began Mama Rat, but the fat man wasn't listening.

'Don't you tell me to calm down! You lot don't know where your bread's buttered, that's the problem. You don't appreciate who feeds and houses you, who pays for your comforts. Without me, you'd all be out on the streets, begging for crusts and offal. But do I get any thanks? No! All I get are shoddy performances and flagrant breaking of my rules. No respect! No respect!'

'You'll be respecting my fist in a minute,' said Gigantus, under his breath. Mama Rat put a restraining hand on his arm.

'What's that?' Plumpscuttle screamed, sending a cascade of spittle into the air. 'Think I'm afraid of you, do you? You great, lumpy oaf! You might be able to crush me like a ripe tomato, but if you do I'll have you thrown into the darkest cell in Newgate prison. And the rest of your little friends will be homeless. Don't think I can't find more freaks . . . and better ones too. Now get on with your chores, and do them *silently*. If one little sound wakes me up, you're all out of here!'

With a final glare, he turned and stamped back into the house, making plaster crumble from the ceiling.

'Well, that was awkward,' said Monkeyboy, when he was sure Plumpscuttle had gone.

'One of these days . . .' Gigantus flexed his arms, and Sheba could hear the threads in his woollen jersey strain and pop.

'I know, dearie,' said Mama Rat. 'But for now let's just keep the peace, shall we?'

'What about the monster crab?' Sheba asked. 'It sounds like it could be a machine.'

'It still not explain why someone taking poor river children,' said Sister Moon.

'No, but it could be *how* they're taking them. And if we could find out where the crab machine is . . .'

'Now, now, Sheba,' said Mama Rat. 'Don't get too carried away. It might be a lead, that's true, but there's not a lot we can do about it at the moment. I suggest we lay low here for a few hours. At least until old grumpychops has gone to sleep properly.'

With a frustrated sigh, Sheba went to fetch the shovel and muck out Flossy.

Monkeyboy waited until the others were all busy, then slipped off to his favourite perch on the roof, a peaceful little spot next to the chimney stack. There was no way he was shovelling sheep crap or shampooing rats. He'd much rather sit up here. He was always more comfortable among the tiles than down on the cobbles. And it was a brilliant position for sniping with one of his hand-rolled poo-balls, like being an archer on a castle turret. His victims usually shouted up to the windows, but never thought of checking the rooftops.

Monkeyboy gazed down at the river of humanity below him – the urchins, the hawkers and the balladeers – leisurely choosing his target. He had a selection of favourite quarry: organ grinders, with their hideous piped music and scrawny little monkeys; stilt-walkers and jugglers, just begging to be knocked over or have their balls sent spinning; and, best of all, the prancing advertising men with their sandwich boards. Monkeyboy had a strong dislike of being told what to do – and what to buy. Especially when he didn't have any money. The men with their sandwich boards and placards irritated him immensely, but the ones that drove him really wild were those idiots in the stupid papier-mâché outfits. He had seen grown men dressed as giant cheeses, colossal boots, massive top hats and even a humungous sausage. All the other pedestrians pointed at them, laughing and clapping, but Monkeyboy knew what they were really up to. They were trying to put images in your head, so you went to their stupid shops and actually bought a cheese, a boot, a top hat or a sausage. When he managed to get a poo-ball inside one of these cramped outfits, it became a super-potent stinkbomb.

A slow smile spread across his face. In the distance, just passing Booth Street, were not one, but two papier-mâché constructions.

Monkeyboy rubbed his hands in glee, then took his stash of ammunition from his pocket and carefully arranged it beside him. If he missed the first one – which looked like a bottle of cough syrup – he would have a crack at the one behind. Goodness only knew what that one was meant to be. It was round and bright orange with a number of huge waving arms, just like a giant octopus. Only its limbs were moving by themselves, powered somehow from within the suit. And from its back jutted a pair of metal pipes, both of which were trickling steam.

Beneath the grime, Monkeyboy's face went pale. The cogs and wheels of thought clunked, slowly linking pieces of information together. Brain cells, previously only used for inventing limericks about bottoms, were applied for the first time to deduction. When he finally realised the importance of what he was looking at, he gave a startled cry and flung himself off the roof and into the street below.

Sheba was just heaving the last of Flossy's dirty hay into the barrow, trying to avoid the little lamb (now back to his gambolling self) as he playfully butted her with both heads, when the yard gate began to rattle with a frantic beating. She dropped the shovel and spun round, just as Gigantus and Sister Moon jumped into fighting stances. Moon had half-drawn her sword when the gate burst open, and the most bizarre hybrid creature toppled in.

The sight of it made Sheba and Mama Rat shriek, and even Gigantus cried out in shock. It was a bright orange contraption with a man's head sticking out of the top and Monkeyboy on the back, whooping like a rodeo rider.

'Get this thing off of me!' cried the man. His eyes were bulging in terror. 'Help me, I'm being attacked!' He spun and whirled, trying to dislodge Monkeyboy, and his suit's many arms flailed about the yard. Gigantus leapt back. Sister Moon dropped and rolled out of the way. Mama Rat's saucepan of water got kicked over, and the rat she was bathing made a dash for freedom.

Finally, Gigantus stepped forward and grabbed hold of the suit. There was a crunching sound as the papier mâché crumpled, but at last the thing was still. The man inside looked as though he was about to either wet himself or be sick, if he hadn't in fact done them both already.

'Monkeyboy, what do you think you're doing?' Mama Rat hissed. 'You're going to wake Plumpscuttle and get us all thrown out.'

'But look!' Monkeyboy shouted. He was pointing to the arms of the suit, which were now feebly clicking and twitching as broken cogs and springs popped out of the joints.

'It's an octopus. We get it,' said Gigantus, looking unimpressed. He was still keeping tight hold of the man's suit.

'It's not just an octopus. It's an octopus *machine*. It's got tubes with steam coming out, just like that boy said. Look! There's writing on the front.'

Beneath the queasy-looking face of the man, words had been painted in bold black across the octopus's chest.

'Guiseppe Farfellini,' Sheba read out. 'Amazing Automata and Incredible Clockwork Creations. Bespoke designs a speciality. Workshop at St Saviour's Dock, Bermondsey.'

'Wasn't St Saviour's where Large 'Arry said the other mudlarks were snatched?' Mama Rat said.

The Peculiars looked at each other. Maybe, just maybe, Monkeyboy had found them a clue. Ignoring the smug look on Monkeyboy's face, Sheba took a step closer to the crab man.

'Do you work for this Farf-el-leenee?' she asked.

The man looked at Sheba and did a double take. He clearly thought he had gone to sleep and was now trapped in some kind of freakish nightmare. 'Yes, yes, I do,' he managed.

'And what kind of . . . *automata* . . . does he make?'

'What? I don't know! Clockwork things that move. Will you let me go and get this crazy brat off of my head! He's put things in my suit – things that *stink*.'

'I'll put a lot more than that in there if you don't start talking,' Monkeyboy whispered into the man's ear. 'I can feel a wee coming on. A *really* big one.'

'Please,' said the man. 'Please. Just let me go. I'm only a sandwich-board man, I don't understand what you want from me.'

'We just want to know something,' Sheba continued. 'Something about your boss. These things he makes . . . have you ever seen one that's a crab? Steam-powered, like the suit you're wearing?'

'I don't know,' said the man, whining now. 'I can't remember.'

'Try harder,' said Gigantus. He gave the suit a squeeze and more cogs sprinkled out from the joints.

There were tears in the man's eyes now. Sheba began to feel sorry for him, but still she had to know.

'I can't remember!' he said. 'There's a workshop, but I've never even been in. I just put on this suit and walk around in it. Now will you please just let me go before I call for the police!'

'I don't think we're going to get much more out of him,' said Mama Rat.

'No,' agreed Sister Moon. 'And he starting to cry.'

'Let him go, Gigantus.' Sheba stood aside as the big man dragged the octopus over to the gate and half-threw it into the street. He pulled the gate shut, just as a series of wet snorts came booming through Plumpscuttle's bedroom window.

The Peculiars huddled together and spoke in whispers.

'Well done, Monkeyboy,' said Sister Moon. 'You find something important.'

'Yes, well spotted, dearie,' agreed Mama Rat.

'All in a day's work,' said Monkeyboy, visibly pleased with himself.

'So, you think this Farty-feely is the one what's been

taking the children?' Gigantus whispered.

'Well, he's a machine-maker with a talent for sea crea-tures,' said Sheba. 'There can't be that many of those in London, can there?'

'So, what we do now?' asked Sister Moon. 'Tell police?'

'Not yet,' said Mama Rat. 'We need proper evidence. We'll have to get a look at this Filly-funny's workshop.'

'Can we go now?' Sheba asked. 'We could be back by showtime?'

'Too risky,' said Gigantus. 'It'll have to wait until tomorrow. Just as long as that whimpering idiot in the octopus suit doesn't go and warn him we're coming. But I think he'll be too scared.'

The others broke from the huddle and went to start preparing the house for that night's show. Sheba was left standing in the yard, still clutching the dirty shovel, almost tempted to rush out of the yard and off to St Saviour's Dock. Except, of course, she had no idea where it was or how to get there. *If you are there, Till, then you'll have to wait for tomorrow. Sorry.*

She just hoped that tomorrow wouldn't be too late.

Chapter Ten

IN WHICH THE PECULIARS GET
A FREE PUPPET SHOW.

Sheba sat looking out from the bedroom window at the twinkling candles of Brick Lane. The fog was especially thick tonight, making the candles seem like will-'o-the-wisps as they shimmered and flickered in little haloes all around her.

From the room behind her came the rumbling of snores. Gigantus and Mama Rat were fast asleep and, judging by the wheezy squeaking sounds coming from the big box, the seven rats were, too. Sheba couldn't help giving a little shudder. Even Sister Moon was dead to the world, lying elegantly on her back with her head on a funny little hard pillow.

Sheba was almost tempted to wake her up. There was no way she could sleep, what with everything running through her head, and she wanted someone to talk to. It made her think back to the long nights at Grunchgirdle's, with the sound of the sea washing back and forth below the floorboards. How she used to slip outside and watch the moon on the waves.

She decided to go and pay Flossy a visit. Sometimes he used to look as though he was listening.

Out in the yard it was dark. She could hear distant shouts, cheers and even screams coming from the Whitechapel streets. Flossy was curled in a little woolly ball, tucked up next to Raggety in the straw. If she hadn't known that horse was a psychopath, she might even have thought he was cuddling him.

Sheba sighed, and wiggled her cold toes on the damp earth. There would be no listening from Flossy, then. She was about to head back inside, when she heard rustling from the direction of Monkeyboy's cage. In the dim light, she could see him sitting up at one end, staring hard at his hands. Dreading what she might see, Sheba moved a little closer.

He was moulding something with his fingers, and as she watched, he set it down on the bars before him. It was a fairly good likeness of the octopus-suited man from earlier, done in earwax and bogies. He regarded it critically for a moment, then sent it spiralling over the fence and into the street with an idle flick.

'Squeal on me to the crushers, will you?' he muttered under his breath.

'The police wouldn't believe him anyway, and Farfellini would probably get rid of him for squealing,' said Sheba. She winced as Monkeyboy jumped with fright and banged his head on the cage roof.

'Sorry,' Sheba said. 'I didn't mean to scare you.'

'Scared? Not likely.' He folded his arms and pouted. 'I knew you was there all along, actually.'

'Of course you did,' said Sheba.

'What you doing out here, anyway?'

Sheba shrugged. 'I couldn't sleep,' she said.

'All that snoring, is it? Keeps me awake, too, when we're out in the caravan. Especially old Lumpy. He sounds like a steam train with asthma.'

'No, not the snoring,' although Sheba did have to agree with him. 'I just keep thinking about Till. About how she might be trapped somewhere, and how we can't do anything to help her.'

'Don't worry.' To Sheba's surprise, he reached out a hand and patted her on the shoulder. 'We'll find her tomorrow, you'll see. My amazing clue will pay off, as sure as Humpty Dumpty doesn't like heights.'

'Thanks, Monkeyboy.' Sheba gave him a smile. 'You're really quite sweet, aren't you?'

'I'm flipping not,' said Monkeyboy. 'And don't go saying stuff like that in public. I have an image to uphold, you know.'

'All right then,' said Sheba. 'It'll be our little secret.' Even in the dim light, Sheba could see he was blushing. Feeling a little better about things, she turned and padded back up to bed.

Not long after dawn the next morning, the Peculiars made their way down from London Bridge, past endless stacks of warehouses and taverns, until they reached a break in the solid mass of buildings.

It looked as if the riverbank had cracked open, letting the water spill in to create a quiet little sidestream. There was barely more than a covering over the mud at the moment, and from it wooden pilings jutted. On top of those, scores of wooden houses had been built, their upper storeys leaning out over the river, as if they were teetering on the verge of falling in. Sheba could see little wooden walkways interlacing the structures.

'St Saviour's Dock,' said Mama Rat. She pointed along the inlet to where brown water gurgled at its mouth. 'That there's the River Neckinger. Flows into the Thames. And over there,' she gestured to a warren of rotten buildings, 'is Jacob's Island.'

'Cholera Island, more like,' said Monkeyboy. 'You'd drop dead soon as you set foot on it.'

Sheba had no intention of going anywhere near it, and she was quite glad when Mama Rat led them around the corner to the Thames. Here were the usual clusters of boats, tied up to a series of rickety pontoons.

In the middle, looming over the other craft, was what

might have been an old warship. Now it was a rotting hulk, stripped of its masts and rigging and left to slowly dissolve in the poisonous water. Faded letters on its stern read HMS *Swiftsure*, but in fresher paint was '*Guiseppe Farfellini, Fabricator of Clockwork and Mechanical Automata Made to Your Precise Specifications. Enquire Within*'. A narrow gangplank led up to a little wooden door, built into the clinkered wood of the hull.

'Well,' said Gigantus, 'it does say "Enquire Within".' And with that he kicked the little door so hard it burst off its hinges.

Mama Rat stayed outside to keep watch, and the rest of the Peculiars made their way onto the ship.

Sheba could feel the boat rocking to and fro on the water, and didn't enjoy the sensation. It seemed oddly familiar to her, although she couldn't think why. As far as she knew, she'd never set foot on a boat before.

Inside the workshop (or workship) was a wide open space with benches lining all the walls. The place was full of powerful aromas: metal, oil, wood shavings and varnish. There were mechanical animals everywhere, and every available surface was covered with tools, parts and sections of half-finished creations. She saw foxes, birds, butterflies, crocodiles, lobsters and turtles. Some of them were so intricate and beautiful, she couldn't help but admire Farfellini's skill. But had he turned it to poor use? She couldn't see anything that looked like a crab. The biggest pieces in the room were two giant wooden puppets. Bearded and dressed in chainmail and helmets, they seemed to be medieval warriors. One held a ball and chain; the other a shield and spear. The wood was bare, as if awaiting a coat of paint, and Sheba could see metal cogs and ratchets gleaming at the joints.

'Gog and Magog,' said Gigantus, sounding impressed.

'Who are they supposed to be?' Sheba asked.

'They're the guardians of London,' said Gigantus. 'It's an old legend, but they have puppets of them in the Lord Mayor's Parade every year.'

'Maybe that's what these are for,' suggested Monkeyboy.

A heavy door at the far end of the room opened, and a little man dashed out. He had olive skin and quick, dark eyes. He was wearing a waistcoat with countless pockets, each holding tools. Sheba spotted tiny pliers, tweezers, rolls of wire and clippers, and cutters of all sizes.

'What is this?' he cried. 'What do you *ruffiani* do to my door?'

'Where is it, puppet man?' Gigantus demanded. 'Where's the machine?'

'What machine? My boat is full of-a machines!'

'The crab machine,' said Sheba. 'The one that's been snatching children from the river.'

Farfellini blinked at them for a moment. His mouth opened and closed soundlessly, as if he was trying to think of something to say. Then he turned and dashed back into his private quarters, slamming the door behind him.

'Well, that's a guilty reaction if ever I saw one,' said Monkeyboy.

'He must have the machine in there!' Sheba shouted.

'Shouldn't be a problem,' said Gigantus. He began to stomp over to the doorway when there was the sound of a loud, metallic clank, followed by a grinding of gears.

'Be careful,' said Sister Moon. 'Little man switch on trap.'

Gigantus stopped. The Peculiars looked warily around them, but the workshop seemed quiet and still. Then a trapdoor in the ceiling slammed open.

Down came a cascade of metal constructions, each one spooling on a length of wire thread. They were the size of saucers: bodies of tin segments, spindly legs jutting and single glowing red eyes. Wind-up keys jutted from their backs, and slung low at the front were long, sharp needles.

'What the hell are those?' shrieked Monkeyboy.

'Spiders,' said Sheba. She could smell the oil and hot metal inside them, and something pungent and chemical that set her fur bristling.

They began to skitter towards the Peculiars. Hard as it was to believe, they seemed to be able to see the intruders.

'Get back,' shouted Sheba, pointing to the mouth-needles. 'They're poisoned, I can smell it.'

Just as they danced away from the creatures, there was another sound from behind them. The Gog and Magog puppets had been activated, and were moving ponderously towards the Peculiars, huge wooden arms swinging like toppling tree trunks. Farfellini must have controls in the other room.

'I take spiders,' Sister Moon called. 'Sheba, you get to puppet man.'

Hurriedly taking some pins from her hair, Sheba ran to the heavy oak door as Gigantus and Monkeyboy turned to face Gog and Magog. Three metres tall, they swung ball and chain, jabbed with shield and spear. They looked like they meant business.

'I'll take the one on the left,' said Gigantus. 'You go for the one with the spear.'

'Me?' shouted Monkeyboy. 'Me? Have you seen the size of me? What am I supposed to do against that thing? It's going to rip me into mincemeat!'

'Stop whining and get on with it.' Gigantus cracked his knuckles, then charged headfirst into Gog, hitting it with a thud that set the whole ship rocking.

'Oh, Mummy!' cried Monkeyboy, but he took a breath and ran at Magog, dodging at the last minute to avoid its spear and scampering up one great oak leg, where he clung on for dear life.

Between the feet of the giant puppets, Sister Moon danced. All around her skittered the little silver spiders, ticking away in a chorus of clockwork. They shot at her legs, trying to stab her with their deadly needles, while their glowing red eyes tracked her every move.

Or tried to, for she was nearly impossible to follow. She leapt and spun in kicks and somersaults, touching the floor for the briefest of instants before flipping somewhere else. Every time she landed, she lashed out with her sword. Each strike hit a target, slicing the legs and bodies of the spiders, until the floorboards were littered with tiny shards of metal.

But still they came at her. One managed to hit her boot, but luckily it missed her toes and shot its lethal payload into the leather of her sole. Another leapt at her, just as she landed from a double backflip. It clung to her belt, and was about to sting her when she knocked it free with her elbow and launched into a spinning front somersault.

Despite the clashes and bangs around her, Sheba tried to focus only on the hairpin in the lock. But it was impossible to ignore the danger her friends were in, and she kept sneaking glances over her shoulder.

Now three of the spiders threatened to jump together on Sister Moon. She couldn't block all of them. Sheba's breath caught. Sister Moon smacked the first away – the other two were raising their needles to strike just as Mama Rat stepped in. She aimed her flintlock pistol and fired, blowing both spiders into shards with one shot. *Where did she learn to shoot like that?* Sheba thought. *And where did that gun come from?* But before she could worry about it any more, her attention was distracted by a roar from across the room.

'Eat this!' Gigantus yelled, slamming another fist into Gog's chest. There was a splintering sound, and a crack finally appeared in the hard oak. The puppet responded with a blow to Gigantus's stomach that knocked him back a step, but it only halted him for a second. 'Monkeyboy, find a way to turn these things off!' he roared, as he started pummelling again.

'How?' Monkeyboy wailed.

Sheba held her breath as he clambered up the puppet's

leg and squeezed inside. A moment later, there came a series of grinding crunches, and the huge model stopped. Monkeyboy's head popped out of the puppet's bottom.

'Oi, lumpy!' he called to Gigantus. 'You can turn it off inside!'

Gigantus gave a nod, and then drove his fist through the cracked chestpiece of Gog and grabbed a handful of metal parts, ripping them free with a crunch. The puppet juddered and froze, a statue once more.

Sister Moon descended from a double backflip to land squarely on the last spider's back. It flew into pieces with a crunch.

'Nice move, Moonie,' Monkeyboy said.

'Rolling porcupine flip. I invent myself.'

Breathing a sigh of relief, Sheba turned back to the lock. She could feel the tumbler beginning to spring. She levered it up, then stuck a second pin into the keyhole to shoot the bolt back. She was rewarded with a loud clunk, and the heavy door swung open a couple of centimetres.

'Oh no you-a don't,' said a voice from inside.

Farfellini's hand shot out, grabbed Sheba's shoulder and pushed hard, flipping her head over heels.

'Sheba!' cried Mama Rat.

Landing on all fours, Sheba turned on the puppet maker, as full of fierce anger as she had ever been. She saw the little man had pulled a strange-looking pistol from his jacket, and was raising it to point at her, but she was too furious to be frightened. This horrid puppeteer had just tried to hurt her friends, and could even have Till hidden away in his room. More than anything, she wanted to teach him a lesson. Her sharp teeth were bared in a snarl, her fingernails had squeezed themselves into sharp little claws, and she knew her eyes were flashing bright orange. *I've never changed this much before,* she thought. *What happens if I can't change back?*

Behind her she heard a roar. It was Gigantus, stampeding towards the door. Farfellini switched aim to the lumbering giant and fired.

There was a *twang*, and Gigantus halted, slapping a hand to his neck as if he'd been stung. A tiny dart with bright red fletchings jutted between his fingers.

Farfellini frantically wound the mechanism on the side of the pistol, getting ready for another shot, just as Mama Rat was pouring powder into the muzzle of her pistol across the room. But Sister Moon was quicker than both. She pulled her sword scabbard from her back and flung it at the man, knocking the gun from his grip and sending it spinning across the floor towards Sheba.

Even as Farfellini made a grab for it, Sheba snatched it up and pointed it straight at his head.

'Don't move, or I'll shoot,' she said. She was still in the grip of her wolfish anger, so the words came out as a kind of snarl.

'Don't-a shoot! Don't-a shoot! Is poison, you silly girl. It kill me!' Farfellini put both hands in the air, as the Peculiars surrounded him.

'What kind of poison?' Sheba asked. 'What have you done to our friend?'

Farfellini looked over to where Gigantus was still clasping his neck, swaying to and fro and looking very pale. 'Nothing bad,' he said, unconvincingly. 'He be fine.'

'No, he pigging won't,' said Monkeyboy.

And they all watched as the big man let out a groan and collapsed to the floor like a felled redwood tree.

While Mama Rat saw to Gigantus and Sister Moon tied up Farfellini, Sheba went to investigate the room where Farfellini had been hiding. Behind her, she could hear Gigantus groaning and the puppeteer cursing in Italian as Monkeyboy interrogated him by using a pair of his pliers to pluck out his nose-hairs one by one.

Farfellini's quarters were quite different from the workshop outside. There was carpet on the floor, pictures on the walls (mostly badly painted views of foreign cities that Sheba assumed were in Italy), a small cot and a stove. There was also a drawing board by the window, and another workbench. Sheba saw several half-built clockwork spiders, just like the ones that had attacked them. By the door was a board covered with levers and wires. Something inside it made it spark and crackle. Electricity, she realised. *The new miracle energy. It must be how he activated his trap.* It was incredible, really. Like magic.

There was no sign of anything crab-like, though. No claws or pincers, no rubber piping or steam engines. Had they jumped to a false conclusion? But he had run away when they'd mentioned a crab — and he had tried to kill them with pistols and poisonous spiders. *There must be something,* Sheba thought. She went to the drawing board. Stacked upon it were sheet upon sheet of detailed drawings. It seemed that Farfellini meticulously planned his every creation.

Sheba saw blueprints for everything in the main room, including Gog and Magog and the spiders, and for others that either weren't here or had yet to be built. There was a tiger, a dragon, an elephant, tiny fairies and a monstrous snake. She was nearing the end of the pile and about to give up when she saw it: the unmistakable shape of a serrated claw.

Throwing the other sketches to the floor, she stretched out the broad sheet of paper and held it up to the light. The design showed a huge contraption with two colossal claws, a series of spindly legs and some kind of screw propeller to drive it through mud. There was also a porthole at the front, surrounded by tiny gaslights. It had a steam engine slotted into the rear, with pipes and vents jutting from under the carapace. And where its stomach should be was a chamber. 'Big enough for two' was scrawled upon it.

'Found anything?' Mama Rat had poked her head around the door into the workshop, and was looking at Sheba expectantly.

Sheba held up the plan and grinned. 'Jackpot,' she said.

Back in the workshop, Gigantus was still sitting with his head in his hands. Mama Rat had managed to remove the dart, and now the big man was quietly groaning while Monkeyboy tenderly patted him on the back. Sister Moon had the point of her sword at Farfellini's throat.

'What you do to my work?' Farfellini managed to croak, raising himself on one elbow. 'You ruin my machines, you steal from my workshop! I call the police, you all go to gaol.'

'Call the police, by all means,' said Mama Rat. 'And then maybe you could explain this to them.' She waved the crab blueprint in his face, and Sheba noticed that he instantly began to tremble.

'That is nothing,' he said. 'Just a design. An idea, only.'

'That's funny,' said Sheba. 'Because a machine *exactly like that one there* has been stealing children from the river.'

'It not prove anything . . .' Farfellini began.

'Well, shall we turn it over to Scotland Yard and see what they make of it, then?' Mama Rat said. 'Or would you like to tell us exactly who you made it for?'

'I can't tell!' Farfellini cried. He was beginning to panic. 'A man come. He pay me. He not say his name.'

'Not good enough,' said Sister Moon. She pushed the sword a little harder into the soft skin of the little man's throat.

'He was a skinny man, *calvo* . . . bald, with spectacles. He give me orders, but that is all, I swear to Santa Maria!'

Sheba and Sister Moon looked at each other. Mama Rat nodded at them, and Sister Moon put her sword away.

'What will you do with me now?' Farfellini asked. His face was white as a sheet.

'I have an idea,' said Gigantus. The big man had managed to get to his feet, but he looked almost as shaky as Farfellini. He wobbled across the workshop, reached down and hoisted up the puppeteer by his throat, until the two were face to face.

'You and I are going for a little walk together,' Gigantus said, growling, and hauled him off the ship.

'I think we should be off, too,' said Mama Rat. 'The peelers could well be on their way here after all the racket we just made.'

Sheba nodded, and they began to make their way out onto the street when she felt something heavy in the pocket of her cloak. She reached a furry little hand inside and pulled out Farfellini's clockwork pistol. She must have tucked it in there and then forgotten about it. She thought about dropping it on the floor. After all, it wasn't really hers. But then again, it might prove useful in a tight spot.

Finders, keepers, she thought, and slipped it back into her pocket before following the others back to Brick Lane.

Chapter Eleven

IN WHICH SHEBA SAMPLES THE
SEEDIER SIDE OF LONDON.

A few hours later Sheba was busy showing everyone the clockwork pistol she had 'found'. Sister Moon popped open the breech, showing her where the darts were loaded. There was a circular spool of little rings that held six shots. One chamber was empty, but the others still held small poisoned thorns with red fletchings, just like the one that had ended up in Gigantus's neck.

'I can make more for you, very easy,' she said. 'I even do range of poisons if you like. Some for sleeping, some for paralysing, some for making blood come out of eyeballs.'

'Um . . . thank you,' said Sheba.

It was just then that the door opened, and a queasy-looking Gigantus staggered in. Sheba quickly hid the pistol away, guessing he probably wouldn't want to be reminded of it. 'My head . . .' he groaned, slumping into a chair. His scarred face had a definite greenish tinge, and beads of sweat covered his brow.

'You poor thing,' said Mama Rat, fetching him a cloth. 'That nasty little puppet man poisoned you good and proper.'

'That poison kill normal-size man,' said Sister Moon.

'Thank goodness you're such a great lump,' said Mama Rat, mopping his forehead.

Gigantus moaned in agreement.

'What exactly did you do with him, by the way?' Sheba asked. She hoped it wasn't anything too horrid.

'Mr Farmy-flanelly is now on a one-way trip to Australia,' muttered Gigantus, holding his head in his hands.

'Transported to the prison colonies?' Mama Rat said, in surprise. 'How did you manage to get him into court so quickly?'

'I didn't,' Gigantus said. 'I just nailed him into a packing crate and paid someone to stick him on the next ship out there. Serves him right for shooting me with that stupid gun.'

Then he groaned again, and made a sound as though he was going to be sick. Sister Moon ran to get a bowl from the kitchen.

'Why don't you lot go out somewhere?' said Mama Rat, looking concerned. 'I think things here are about to turn a spot unpleasant. I'll send my ratties along with you to keep you safe.'

'Right you are,' said Monkeyboy, not needing to be told twice. He was out of the front door in a few seconds, and Sheba and Sister Moon followed close behind.

'We're best off out of there,' said Monkeyboy, when they were safely on the street. 'Can you imagine that huge gorilla throwing up? It'd be like a tidal wave of spew. We'd probably have drowned in half-chewed mutton.'

'Enough, Monkey,' said Sister Moon. 'At least we have afternoon for ourself. Where shall we go?'

'We could go to the Great Exhibition,' suggested Sheba. 'You did say we would, and I'd love to see the Crystal Palace and the big diamond.'

'Too expensive,' said Sister Moon, looking at the few coins in the pouch on her belt. 'We not have three shillings.'

'What about the Penny Gaff down the road? They're a steaming great heap of bum-juice but they do an afternoon show most days,' Monkeyboy said. 'We've got plenty enough for that, and some cakes and lemonade besides.'

Sheba and Sister Moon agreed, and the three of them set off.

Sheba pulled her hood down over her eyes, and kept her hands tucked beneath her cloak. Monkeyboy had hidden his tail down a trouser leg and jammed his battered top hat over his huge ears. Oddly enough, Sister

Moon was the one getting all the stares. Probably because she was a girl wearing trousers.

Through the door behind them, a nasty retching sound could be heard. Sheba trotted a little faster, just in case Monkeyboy was right, and a giant wave of vomit was about to chase them down the street.

Back in Little Pilchton, Sheba had read about Penny Gaffs in scraps of newspaper, which described them as dens of vice and criminal behaviour. Officially they were cheap versions of the theatre, with a range of badly performed acts that kept their rowdy audiences entertained for an hour or so. Of all the sights she had wanted to see in London, it wasn't very high on her list.

'I'm sure going to a Penny Gaff will be interesting,' she said, politely as they walked along Cable Street.

'You clearly haven't been to one before,' Monkeyboy cackled.

'Where are rats?' Sister Moon asked. 'I not see them.'

Sheba sniffed the air. There were scents of rodent every-where, but then there were probably more rats in London than people.

'I think we've lost them,' she said.

'Good,' said Monkeyboy. 'Them things give me the creeps.'

They turned on to the Ratcliff Highway. It was a seedy, dirty place, with people lying in the gutter and hordes of ragged children leaping around piles of rotting litter. The smell of disease and decay made Sheba feel sick, and she took her handkerchief out and held it to her nose.

'Lovely here, innit?' said Monkeyboy, grimacing. 'Just the place for an afternoon out. Makes Brick Lane look like bleeding Mayfair.'

'This the place,' said Sister Moon. She had stopped by an ancient, timber-fronted building that looked as though it might have once been an inn. The outside was covered with pasted playbills, all too weather-stained to read.

'I'll say it again,' said Monkeyboy. 'I hope you're not expecting anything spectacular. I don't want the blame if it's rubbish.'

'It be good, Monkey. You see.' Sister Moon ducked through the low door, not waiting for the others to follow. Suddenly, without a *ninja* to protect them, the Highway didn't seem a very safe place for two young children to be standing. Monkeyboy and Sheba quickly followed.

They came out into a small, crowded tavern. Sheba could smell lots of unwashed bodies, pipe smoke and gin, and also something sweet. Over in the corner she saw a makeshift bar, where a woman was selling apples and slices of unhealthy-looking cake.

Sister Moon was standing at the far doorway, beckoning. It looked as though the show was about to start. Sheba and Monkeyboy pushed through the unwashed bodies towards her. As they arrived she dropped three pennies into the hand of the doorman and they went through into the theatre.

It was dark inside, and even smellier than the tavern.

People were squashed into the small pit area next to the stage, and it was with difficulty that the three of them managed to push their way through to the rows of wooden benches at the back, which stretched up to the ceiling like a Roman amphitheatre (if amphitheatres had been knocked together by a few drunken carpenters out of worm-eaten timber). Sister Moon grabbed hold of a wonky ladder and scampered right to the top, where she found an empty bench. Monkeyboy followed, just as agile, but Sheba found the climb difficult and not a little frightening.

After minutes of clutching the splintered rungs and praying she wouldn't fall onto the heads of the crowd beneath, she felt Sister Moon's hands around her wrists, lifting her up. Stress had made her claws come out, and she left little gouge marks on the top rung. They had a bird's-eye view of the whole theatre. The stage below seemed small, but at least the air was clearer up here, away from all the dirty clothes and festering armpits.

A little man came out onto the stage. There was an immediate roar from the audience, and it was very hard to hear what he was saying. It sounded as if he was boasting of the marvels of his show – a bit like Plumpscuttle did every night before their own performances.

The more the man went on, the more the crowd jeered. At one point, he compared his theatre to the Great Exhibition, and the whole audience fell about laughing. He seemed to take that as the final straw, and disappeared through a trapdoor in the stage floor.

There was a brief moment of silence from the crowd, then a lady in an extraordinary amount of petticoats came on. There were wolf whistles and cheers, some rather pleasant music started – played by three men at the corner of the stage – and she began to dance.

She wasn't the most agile or slender of dancers, unfortunately, and soon the audience in the pit were throwing things at her. Eventually, she was booed off, and the director edged on stage again to announce his next act.

'Ladies and Gentlefolk, may I now present to you the scientific genius, Mr Faraday!'

The audience shrieked and booed as a man in a black suit and enormous wig of wild grey hair came on. He carried a badly painted box, covered with coiling copper wires, strange dials and a crank handle on the side, which he placed on a small table and pretended to tinker with.

'What's a scientific genius doing in a place like this?' Sheba shouted into Sister Moon's ear, trying to make herself heard over the noise.

'It not really him,' Sister Moon yelled back. 'Is actor. Is famous because of new invention.'

Sheba was about to ask what he had invented, but the performance on stage soon made it clear. As he turned the handle, his box exploded with a bang and the actor jittered about the stage as if being shocked, before collapsing in a smoking heap. The crowd threw empty bottles and apple cores at the stage, forcing the man to scramble away on all fours.

'He made something electric, did he?' Sheba thought

of the board of levers and wires on Farfellini's ship.

'He very clever scientist,' said Sister Moon. 'You not heard of him?'

Sheba shrugged, not knowing how to explain the patchy nature of her general knowledge. *As soon as I get a chance, I'm going to buy myself an encyclopedia*, she thought.

When the interval came, Sheba was rather relieved. Monkeyboy went off to get some cake for them all, leaving her to enjoy the relative peace and quiet.

'Is something the matter, Sheba?' asked Sister Moon. 'You not like the show?'

'It's all right, I suppose,' said Sheba. 'Not my sort of thing, really.'

'Yes. In Japan we have theatre called *kabuki*. It more civilised than this.'

'Do you miss your home?' she asked. What had driven the young girl so far from her native country?

'A lot, yes.' Sister Moon looked suddenly very sad.

'I'm sorry,' she said. 'I didn't mean to remind you.'

'Don't worry,' Sister Moon forced herself to smile. 'I cannot go back there, so I must get used to the sadness.'

'Why not?' asked Sheba. 'Why can't you return?'

Sister Moon paused for a moment, thinking. Obviously this was something serious, and she was wondering whether to trust Sheba or not. When she spoke again, Sheba felt a rush of affection – that she had been deemed worthy to share Sister Moon's secret.

'In Japan I do bad things, Sheba. Things I not proud of.' She halted, looking around to see if anyone was listening.

When she next spoke, it was almost in a whisper.

'I work for a group called Shadow Fist. We belong to powerful shogun as ninja . . . assassin. My master, he train me for many years, make me the best of all his ninja. But then one day he give me new task. He ask me to kill daughter of rival shogun. A girl not much younger than me.'

Sister Moon stopped; pressed her hands to her eyes for a moment. Sheba put an arm round her and squeezed gently.

'I refuse,' said Sister Moon. 'I refuse mission. Bring disgrace to Shadow Fist. In my country, if you do such a thing, is terrible crime. My master would have had to kill me. So I leave. Get on first boat and come here. Monkeyboy and Gigantus find me in Whitechapel, save me from attack by gang. Mama Rat persuade Plumpscuttle to take me.'

For a moment, Sheba didn't know what to say. Finally, she took one of Sister Moon's hands in hers.

'You poor thing,' she said. Then, because that sounded so hopelessly inadequate: 'Your master, he sounds like a horrid man. It's good that you got away from him.'

'He horrid man . . . but . . . he my father.'

There was an awkward silence, broken by Monkeyboy returning with the cake.

'What's going on here?' he said. 'Heart to heart, is it? Has Moonie told you her sad story?'

'Shut up, Monkeyboy,' said Sheba. She didn't mean to be so harsh, but she was feeling responsible for opening Sister Moon's old wound, and also dredging up thoughts of her own lost family.

'Wait till you hear my story, then. It makes hers sound like a comedy.' Monkeyboy finished his mouthful of cake and handed the rest around. Then he cleared his throat, as if about to launch into a performance of his own.

'I was born on a boat, I was,' he said. 'A transportation ship, on its way back from Australia with those what had served their time. My mam was aboard, heavy with child (which was me, of course). They were just passing the Isle of Wight when she gave birth. A strange little thing with a tail. Everyone screamed in terror and thought it was a bad omen – the ship was going to sink and all that – so they wrapped me up and threw me overboard.'

Sheba wasn't sure whether to believe any of this. She looked across at Sister Moon, who appeared to be taking it seriously.

'Days and nights I must have drifted on the sea, until I washed up on a Cornish beach. The local tavern-keeper took me in, and that's where I grew up. Hanging in a cage and forced to sing rude limericks to all the pirates and smugglers. And I'd be there still, if old Plumpscuttle hadn't come by one day. Just lost his fortune when his boat sank on the way back from America. Bet all he had left on a game of blackjack and won the jackpot . . . me! I was his first freak, I was. Just goes to show, when one door closes, another one opens.'

Monkeyboy bowed as if he'd just done a Penny Gaff act of his own.

'Were you really his first freak?' Sheba asked.

'I certainly was!' Monkeyboy reached across and took

her uneaten piece of cake, cramming it into his mouth in one go. 'He had a couple more after me: a grumpy little dwarf and some bloke who said he was older than Julius Caesar. They didn't hang around for long, though. Then he found Mama Rat and Gigantus, straight off a boat from France, and the rest is history!'

Sheba wanted to ask more – such as, what were Mama Rat and Gigantus doing in France? – but the audience had started shrieking again. It was time for the main perform-ance, which turned out to be some kind of bizarre story of a man who kept escaping from prison by tying bedsheets together and picking locks. He wasn't even doing it right, Sheba noticed in disgust.

'What's all this about?' she asked, as the hero was being chased around the stage by an angry mob.

'Story of Jack Sheppard,' said Monkeyboy, 'most famous jailbreaker in the world. Robbed from the rich, broke the hearts of half the dollymops in London and escaped from every lock-up they held him in. Nobody ever told him what to do. My hero.'

It was all about as well-acted as a Punch and Judy show, but the crowd seemed to love it. They whooped and cheered so loudly it made Sheba's ears ring. Monkeyboy was actually doing backflips of excitement on the bench next to her.

Then it was all over. The roars began to subside and everyone suddenly stood up.

'We go now,' Sister Moon said. 'Owner cross if you not get out quick. They want to make room for next audience. Take more money that way.'

Sheba noticed the director had returned, this time with a pair of very large bouncers. The rest of the crowd was making for the door as fast as the crush allowed.

With Sister Moon helping, Sheba scrambled down the ladder as quickly as she could. The three of them plunged into the throng and, holding hands tightly, were somehow swept along, through the door and into the street outside.

'Crikey,' said Sheba, as she rearranged her cloak. 'Isn't there a better way of getting out of the place?'

One of the unspoken laws of London was that, as soon as three or more people stood still for more than a minute, a horde of street vendors and ballad singers would descend on them like a swarm of flies on a fresh pile of manure. The crowd that had previously been the audience now filled the street, and as if a secret signal had gone out, they were suddenly set upon by jugglers, card-sharps and gypsies, all trying to squeeze some extra pennies out of them.

Sheba and the others dodged a ballad-singer, a clothes-peg-hawker and an acrobat before they were finally cornered by a mad-looking old woman with filthy grey hair and no teeth. She shoved a basket of rotten pastries at them and screeched in a broken voice.

'Pork pie, luvvie? Pig in a blanket?'

Sheba stepped back from the reeking meat, just as a gang of small children bustled past. Monkeyboy instantly hopped in front of her and shouted over his shoulder.

'Watch your pockets! They're dippers, and she's their kidsman!'

Sheba wondered for a moment what language he was speaking, and then realised he was talking about the children picking her pockets. She was about to tell him she had nothing worth taking, when she remembered the clockwork pistol and Till's marble. Her hands flew to the pouches in her cloak lining. Thankfully, everything was still there. The hideous old pie woman screeched something unintelligible at them and spat on the cobbles.

'Sling yer hook, you smelly old hag!' Monkeyboy shouted after her.

Sister Moon looked at the crowd around them, frowning. 'This not good place,' she said. 'We go before more trouble.'

Sheba agreed. It was getting later in the day, and this wasn't a place to spend a pleasant evening. Not unless you enjoyed getting robbed, murdered and robbed again. She was about to follow the others back to Brick Lane when she caught sight of something in the doorway of the inn across the road. Suddenly, her feet became rooted, her hair bristling all over her body.

'Sheba, we must go,' Sister Moon repeated, grabbing hold of her arm, then she stopped.

'What is it?' Sheba asked.

'Over there,' Sister Moon whispered. 'In the doorway.'

There were several figures lounging about the tavern door, every one of them looking like they would happily slit your throat for tuppence. But one in particular stood out.

He was wearing a long, dark coat, and matted locks of hair trailed down his back from beneath his hat. He was talking intensely to two terrifying-looking goons – one with a bushy black beard and another with a blood-spattered butcher's apron. Although he stood within the shadows of the doorway, Sheba could still see the intricate pattern of coal-black stripes and swirls on his face. And there was a hint of something else in the air – oil and spice. She gasped.

'Man at graveyard,' hissed Sister Moon. 'I sure.'

'And his face, the patterns. It's what Barney Bilge said he saw in the crab machine's eye! How many people in London have painted faces like that?'

Monkeyboy, having walked twenty metres down the road before realising the others weren't with him, scampered back to them. 'What's the hold-up?' he said. 'We should be hooking it out of here, not standing around taking the flipping air.'

Abruptly the painted stranger finished speaking, then nodded and left the tavern doorway, turning right along Ratcliff Highway.

'We have to follow him,' Sheba said. Something in her gut told her this man had something to do with the missing mudlarks. She could almost smell it.

'Follow that?' Monkeyboy goggled down the street after the stranger. 'You must be joking. He looks like he'd pop our eyeballs out, just for a laugh.'

'I not sure about this, Sheba. Not on our own—'

But before Sister Moon could finish, Sheba was off through the crowd, following the spice-and-oil scent of the stranger like a two-legged bloodhound. Monkeyboy and Sister Moon shared a stricken glance before dashing after her.

They happened to have forgotten all about their ratty escort. It was lucky that Mama Rat's babbies, scuttling along the gutters and rooftops after them, had better memories.

Chapter Twelve

IN WHICH SHEBA HAS A CLOSE SHAVE.

They followed the painted man along the highway, past St Katherine's Docks and out of the East End. All the while they kept as far behind as they could without losing sight of him. Every now and then, Sister Moon would push them into a doorway or behind a hawker's street-stall. Split seconds later, the man would turn and glare back up the road, but see nothing. *It's almost as if she* knows *when he's about to look round*, Sheba thought. She supposed stalking people must be part of an assassin's training.

They walked past the piece of old wall that marked

the edge of Roman Londinium and alongside the Tower of London. Sheba shivered as she passed it, imagining swirls in the mist were the ghosts of beheaded prisoners watching them. London Bridge was crowded with hansom cabs, carts and horses and scores of people in between, hurrying to get away from the stink of the Thames.

Once over the river, they headed down Tooley Street, holding their breath for as long as they could past the tanning yards. Once or twice they lost sight of the painted man in the crowds, but Sheba still had a hold of his scent. She followed it as if it were an invisible rope.

He led them through a maze of streets, past docks and warehouses, and on to a wide, cobbled road. It looked as if it might once have been a grand place to live. On either side stood three-storey stone houses with high, square windows and tall chimneystacks. Most had steps up to the front doors. But the painted doors were peeling, the sagging roofs were shedding slates like autumn leaves, and the windows were cracked and filthy.

'If we're not back soon, Plumpscuttle is going to skin us alive,' said Monkeyboy.

'Quiet,' hissed Sister Moon. 'Man stopping.'

The three of them ducked into a nearby doorway and watched as the painted man walked up the stone steps of one house and pulled on the bell. There was a moment's pause before the door opened and a tiny little man stepped out. He had scrawny limbs and an oversized head. A white frizz jutted out around his ears, but there was no hair anywhere else on the bulging dome of his skull. He also wore a pair of thick, heavy glasses.

Sheba's heart was in her throat. She whispered to the others, 'Remember what Farfellini said about the man who gave him the order for the crab?'

'Skinny,' said Monkeyboy.

'Bald,' said Sister Moon.

'And spectacles,' added Sheba. 'Exactly.'

The two men shook hands, then walked inside the house. As the slam of the door echoed down the street, Sheba and the others stepped out of their hiding place.

'That's it,' she said. 'We've found them. They must be the ones who've taken Till. She could even be inside that house right now.'

'Number 17,' Sister Moon said, peering down the street at the house. 'We go back and tell Mama Rat what we find.'

Something about the number made Sheba pause. She looked around the road for a street sign, finally spotting one screwed to the side of a building behind them. *Paradise Street*.

'What is it, hairy?' asked Monkeyboy. 'You look like someone's just stuck a rat down your knickers.'

'17 Paradise Street,' Sheba replied. When the others looked at her blankly, she drew out the pasteboard calling card from her cloak pocket.

The house was Mrs Crowley's.

* * *

'She knows them, the sneaky witch!' Monkeyboy's face boggled and bulged as he slowly became more outraged. 'She was stringing us along from the start!'

Sheba frowned. The dilapidated house didn't seem to fit with the fine quality of clothes Mrs Crowley wore, or her clipped accent. Somewhere, a ship's horn sounded. The river where Mrs Crowley's son had supposedly gone missing wasn't far. Could her posh façade have been an act? Could her child have been a mudlark, too?

'They might be helping her look for her son,' Sheba suggested. 'There might be an innocent explanation.'

'Too much of a coincidence,' said Monkeyboy. 'Those two have got something to do with the missing mudlarks.'

Sister Moon looked as puzzled as Sheba. 'Maybe they giving her son back? Or asking her for ransom?'

'Or maybe they've got the mudlarks tied up in the basement somewhere and they're about to eat them for supper?'

Beneath her hood, Sheba's face was set in a determined scowl. 'There's only one way to find out.'

'What you think?' Sister Moon asked. 'That we break in house?'

Sheba nodded, and Monkeyboy let out a whimper. 'You must be crazy,' he said. 'Anyway, we're supposed to be back at Brick Lane any minute. Plumpscuttle will kill us if we're not there for the show — unless those three do it first.'

'We'll be quick,' said Sheba. 'If we don't hear anything

about Till, we'll be out again and on our way home straight away.'

'But we're bound to get caught,' Monkeyboy whined. 'Caught and thrown in a dungeon somewhere.'

'Do what I tell you, Monkey,' said Sister Moon. 'I expert sneak. We go in at back.'

The three mismatched figures scurried around behind the row of houses and found an alley. It was narrow and dark, with splintered fences close on both sides. When Sister Moon stepped into it, she seemed to disappear, the white skin of her face appearing to float in the gloom.

'Come on,' she whispered. 'No time to slither.'

'Dither,' corrected Sheba, joining her in the shadows.

Monkeyboy stood for a moment on his own, quietly snivelling, before one of Sister Moon's arms reached out from the alley and yanked him in.

A few moments later, they were standing at the back door of number 17. Nobody had rushed out to seize them yet. The small garden around them was a mass of weeds and brambles, another sign of dilapidation that didn't fit with Mrs Crowley.

Sheba heard a church clock strike six somewhere in the distance, as she worked on the back door lock. They really would have to be quick if they were to get back in time for the show at eight. She hoped there weren't any dead-bolts besides the clunky old keyplate she was picking.

The thought of the painted man being just behind the door made her breath catch in her throat. If they were caught, what would happen? Her hand shook, rattling the picks against the lock. She forced herself to take some deep breaths and tried again. This time, the tumbler clicked into place and the door swung silently open.

They entered a dark and empty kitchen. The house beyond it was silent and still. There was something unnatural about being in someone else's house uninvited. They tiptoed through the room and started up what would have been the servants' staircase. Sister Moon led the way, with Monkeyboy clinging to her shoulders. Sheba followed, trying to put her feet exactly where Moon had. Every time the stairs made a tiny creak, her heart nearly stopped beating.

The whole place was dark, yet somehow Sister Moon moved with confidence, as if it were broad daylight. *Must be her cat's eyes*, thought Sheba, remembering how Sister Moon's eyes had shrunk to slits that first night in the caravan. Even with her own wolfish senses, Sheba could only pick out dim outlines of the walls and stairs, but she could smell mildew, dust and woodworm: neglect.

When they got to the second floor, they stepped onto a wide landing in the main part of the house. It was lit only by a flickering gaslight. The paper on the walls was yellowed with age, and the floorboards were scuffed and warped. There were no grand paintings, no potted plants and ornaments. The place was bare. If it hadn't been for the dim murmur of voices in a room somewhere, she would have thought it derelict and abandoned.

They silently made their way down the landing to the

source of the noise. And stopped by a heavy oak door, which gleamed with light at the cracks. There were voices inside – two or three people at least. Sheba looked at the others, wide-eyed. Her bravado had now completely evaporated, and she realised she was standing in a stranger's house, a couple of metres away from the owner herself, and possibly two very nasty villains. She motioned back down the stairs, meaning: *I really, really think we should go now.*

Sister Moon shook her head. She pointed to the keyhole and held her fingers to her eye in a circle. Then she pointed to Sheba.

Why me? Sheba mouthed, but it was obvious. She had the best hearing, and she might also be able to pick up a scent through the tiny hole. Sister Moon and Monkeyboy edged back along the landing to where another door stood open. *Thanks a bunch,* Sheba thought, but she bent her head to the keyhole.

Although her field of view was limited, she could see a thick, musty rug, ornate chairs and a chipped sideboard with a tea service on top. On the walls hung two large oil portraits in ornate ebony frames. One was of a beautiful woman, dressed in cascading folds of white silk. The other showed a handsome army officer, hand on sword and with a backdrop of some faraway country. Both were obscured by a thick coating of dust. Mrs Crowley's ancestors, perhaps? Or the people that used to own this crumbling house?

Sheba almost didn't notice Mrs Crowley at first. The

way she sat motionless in a high-backed leather armchair, covered from head to foot with layers of black cloth, made her look like a shrouded statue. The only clue that she wasn't were the white tips of her fingers, which gently twitched on the chair arms as she observed the people standing before her.

One was the painted man. His broad shoulders stretched out the fabric of his coat, and without his hat his locks spilled down his back like greasy rats' tails.

The other figure was the man with the mad, white hair. He wore an old, stained frock coat, and was clearly quite excited about something. He was waving his arms and gesticulating madly.

She was now close enough to pick up their scents. The painted man's spice-and-oil aroma was more like some type of incense, she thought. The other was ripe with some kind of chemical mix. Medical, perhaps. But not the good kind. There was a hint of something noxious beneath: rotten meat, dead things. Both odours set Sheba's hackles on edge. She felt an almost overwhelming urge to turn and run back down the stairs, but somehow she fought it. She had to stay and hear what they were saying.

'Are you sure you will be able to get it?' the small man was asking. 'They have it very well guarded.'

'You just worry about your part,' came the lisping voice of Mrs Crowley. 'Leave the rest to me.'

'Yes, but without it, I will not be able to make it work—'

'Doctor.' Mrs Crowley leant forward in her chair. She

sounded as though her patience was wearing thin. 'I have assured you that I will be able to obtain it.'

Sheba frowned at the keyhole. So the man was a medical doctor. But what was 'it'? What were they after?

'Now, about the children . . .'

Sheba's heart began to beat so loudly, she thought they would be able to hear it on the other side of the door. She had to focus on calming herself so she could pay proper attention again.

'One more should be sufficient,' the doctor was saying. 'If only that last boy hadn't managed to escape.'

'But the tides aren't right tonight.' The painted man's voice rumbled like a brewing thunderstorm. He had a thick, foreign accent; it was not one Sheba could remember hearing before, but for some reason it seemed familiar.

'Very well, Baba Anish. Tomorrow, then. At low tide – just as with the others. Within hours, we shall have what we most desire. And how long we have waited . . .'

That woman, Sheba thought. And to think she had felt sorry for her. There clearly was no lost son. And Mrs Crowley was no grieving mother.

'Yes, but something happened to the puppet maker,' the Doctor said. 'And there's that bunch of freaks looking for one of the children—'

Sheba caught a strong waft of Mrs Crowley's peculiar scent as she jerked forward in her chair. 'The puppet man owed money to some nasty people,' she snapped. 'Why do you think he was so keen to take our coin? They must have lost patience with him in the end. And as for those irritating snoops, they are nothing to worry about. I met them, don't forget. And they were just as stupid as I expected. The woman was clueless, and as for that hideous little girl . . . my Indian friend here has a cure for her.'

The painted man gave a deep chuckle that sounded more like a panther growling. It was followed by the sound of something sharp and metal being drawn from a scabbard. Sheba could suddenly smell dried blood – human blood. Without meaning to, she let out a tiny squeak of terror.

'What was that?' came Mrs Crowley's sharp whisper.

Heavy footsteps began to approach the door. The metal-and-blood stink drew closer and closer. Sheba wanted desperately to run, but for some reason her feet were rooted to the floor.

The door handle began to move, she could see it from the corner of her eye, but still her legs were stuck like stone. *Run, you stupid girl. Run!* she shouted to herself. Where was the wolf when she really needed it?

Just as the door began to creak open, she felt a hand on her shoulder. She looked round.

It was Sister Moon.

Life returned instantly to her limbs. Sheba scampered along the landing and into the room where Monkeyboy was hiding.

Behind her, the door continued to open.

Mrs Crowley called out, 'It's probably just a floorboard, Baba Anish. This dismal place is falling to pieces. Little wonder they left it behind to rot.'

Sheba crouched behind the door of the dark room she had dashed into. Monkeyboy jumped into her arms and she held him in a tight squeeze. She was so scared, she almost didn't notice the smell. Beside her, Sister Moon had dropped to a fighting crouch and was drawing her swords from their scabbards slowly and silently.

Out in the corridor, she heard the man Mrs Crowley had called Baba Anish taking careful steps forward. She imagined his eyes sliding from shadow to shadow like a hawk's, that bloodied weapon ready to slice whatever he found.

She could feel the spicy scent grow stronger and stronger as he approached. *We should have closed the door behind us*, she thought. *We might as well have put a sign outside saying 'We're In Here!'* As the fear and adrenalin built up inside her, Sheba could feel the fur thickening on her face. Claws started to poke from her fingertips, digging into Monkeyboy's back where she held him. He gave a little yelp of pain.

Immediately, the footsteps halted. Baba Anish's breathing paused as he listened. After the longest ten seconds in the history of time, he began to move again. This time there was no doubt he was coming towards their door.

Sister Moon had her swords out now. She gave Sheba a grim look, the slits of her pupils gleaming in the light from the hallway. Sheba's mind raced. Would Moon be able to take Baba Anish on her own? What could she and Monkeyboy do to help?

She was finding it hard to think, as the wolfish instincts started to take over. She couldn't help feeling the urge to rush out and launch herself at Baba Anish, but she knew she would last less than a heartbeat. *Maybe we could escape out of the window*, she thought. *Or Monkeyboy could climb down and get help* . . .

But before anything could happen, there was a squeaking sound at her feet. Her first thought was that she had stepped on a wonky floorboard, but then something black and furry ran across her toes. It dashed past Sister Moon and out through the open doorway, causing Baba Anish to shout in surprise.

One of Mama Rat's babbies!

Sheba felt a brief surge of relief. Until she heard the sound of something sharp swishing down.

Thunk.

There was a shrill squeak, then silence.

'What is it?' came Mrs Crowley's muffled voice from the next room.

'Just a rat,' said Baba Anish. His voice was so loud; he must have been centimetres from the door where the Peculiars were hiding. 'A very big one.'

'A rat? There are no rats in my house!'

More footsteps as Baba Anish returned to the study. Evidently he had taken the rat's body with him, as there was a scream, which Sheba thought was Mrs Crowley.

'It's hideous!' yelled the doctor in a high-pitched voice. 'Take it away this instant! I can't stand rats!'

'I think we should be departing, anyway,' said Mrs

Crowley. 'I'm sure you have final preparations to put in place, and I have some guards to bribe.'

'Yes, yes,' said the doctor. 'Everything will be ready for tomorrow night.'

Footsteps could be heard leaving the room and walking down the main staircase.

The Peculiars didn't move a muscle until they heard the front door shut. There was silence then, but they waited another few minutes to make sure the house was empty. Only then did Sister Moon put her swords away, and Monkeyboy reluctantly peeled himself out of Sheba's arms.

'That poor rat,' whispered Sheba. She felt her eyes begin to prickle with tears. 'Which one was it?'

'It was only a flipping rat,' said Monkeyboy. 'She's got loads more of the creepy things.'

'They very special rats,' whispered Sister Moon. 'They follow us from Penny Gaff. They take care of us. I think that one might be Matthew. He the ringmaster.'

'What are we going to say to her?' Sheba knew how upset Mama Rat would be. The rats were like her babies. And it had been *her* stupid idea to come here. It was her fault one of the rats had been killed. In fact, she had nearly got them all killed.

'Not worry now. We get back for show, or there be even more trouble.'

Sister Moon led the way back down the stairs, the others tiptoeing after. Somehow they made it out through the back door in silence, then began the frantic dash back to Brick Lane.

Chapter Thirteen

IN WHICH PLUMPSCUTTLE GETS A PASTING.

That evening's show was the most dismal ever. Gigantus, still under the effects of Farfellini's poisoned dart, couldn't lift his own feet, let alone anything else. Monkeyboy could barely bring himself to fart a tune, and Sheba spent the entire time trying not to cry. Mama Rat managed to get her rats to put on some semblance of a performance, but there was no ratty ringmaster, and every time she thought about it she burst into sobs. Sister Moon even missed the target with one of her throwing stars and nearly took a customer's nose off.

Sheba felt too guilty to even try to apologise. After the

show was done, after Plumpscuttle had gone, she would find a way of expressing her sorrow to Mama Rat. But before then she had to sit through two long hours of being stared at.

To make matters even worse, Plumpscuttle's nephew made the unfortunate mistake of letting an old lady in for half price.

'I don't care if someone has actually been *chopped in half* – you still charge them the same as everyone else! Do you understand, you snivelling little snot-stain?' Plumpscuttle stomped about in the front room, spittle flying, venting his rage on the Peculiars. His face went a shade of purple Sheba had never seen before.

'I'm sorry, Uncle. Can I go home now?'

'Home? *Home?* I'll send you flipping home!' Plumpscuttle grabbed his nephew by the ear and hoisted him to the front door, which he yanked open with his other hand. Then he booted the boy in the buttocks, sending him flying into the street. There was a fading squeal, followed by a thud. Plumpscuttle slammed the door.

'And as for *you* lot, what in the name of Queen Vic's pyjamas do you call that? Performing rats that can barely do handstands? A strongman who can't even lift an eyebrow? A *ninja* who can't throw straight? A grotesque hidden under a pile of straw and a wolfgirl without so much as a wet nose? I'll tell you what: after I've had my second – no, third – dinner tonight, I'm going to start making enquiries about a new lot of freaks. Ones what do what's flipping well asked of them!'

He gave them all a final glare, then stormed out of the house, banging the door so hard that the windows shook in their frames.

There was silence in the front room for a good few minutes after that. Finally, they moved to huddle round the fireplace. Sheba went to Mama Rat, the tears spilling out of her eyes and soaking into the fur on her cheeks. Getting Matthew killed was the worst thing she'd ever done. Grunchgirdle had beaten her for much less. *Whatever Mama Rat does to me, I deserve it*, she thought.

But Mama just took her by the shoulders and pulled her into a tight hug. Sheba was overcome. It was the first ever hug she could remember. Being so close to someone was overpowering to begin with, but warm and safe as well. She snuggled further into Mama Rat's arms, breathing deep the smell of pipe smoke, lavender and rodent.

'I'm so sorry,' she sobbed into Mama Rat's shoulder.

'It's not your fault, dearie. I know you didn't mean him to come to harm.'

'But you shouldn't have gone off on your own like that,' said Gigantus. 'These are evidently dangerous people we're dealing with.'

'They weren't to know that, were they?' Mama Rat said.

'Even so . . .'

'It my fault,' said Sister Moon. She bowed her head in shame. 'I tell them I know what to do.'

'But it was my idea,' said Sheba. 'If anyone's to blame, it's me.'

'I'd just like to point out that I was against it all along,' said Monkeyboy.

'It doesn't matter whose idea it was,' said Mama Rat. 'The only people to blame are that Crowley woman and her henchmen. How that cold-hearted cow could use the idea of a dead child to trick us . . . Anyway, that's beside the point. The next time you get it into your heads to do something like that, we all go together. Understood?'

The three young Peculiars all nodded their heads sheepishly, before each went to help take down the paraphernalia from the show. By the time they had finished, Sheba felt too tired to think about what they'd learnt at Mrs Crowley's house, too tired even to worry about Till. She left the others sitting around the fireplace and trudged up to the bedroom.

She sat on the edge of her mattress, not knowing what to do with herself. Crawling into bed was tempting, but she knew it would be a long time before she fell asleep. Time which her mind would spend replaying horrid scenes from the evening: the painted man creeping towards her hiding place, the awful sound of his blade slicing through poor Matthew . . .

She needed a distraction. Then she noticed that Gigantus had already rolled out his bedding. Beneath it, the telltale lump of his book could be seen. Perhaps a spot of Agnes Throbbington might cheer her up. Before she could even convince herself it was a bad idea, she had slid the heavy book out and was opening it to a new page.

Agnes strolled along the High Street on a beautiful summer's morning. Her head was dizzy with thoughts, mostly about how extraordinarily beautiful she was. 'I really do deserve to be married to someone incredibly handsome and wealthy,' she said to herself. She was growing bored of Jeremy Gristle. She had been madly in love with him for three whole days now, and she was beginning to tire of the smell of pig.

She scanned the crowds that filled the street. She was looking out for someone worthy enough to admire her. And then she saw him.

Stepping out of a coffee shop, he positively gleamed in his bright red captain's uniform. He had a magnificently manly set of whiskers, and his manly hands had probably slaughtered hundreds of savages.

Agnes's heart did a backflip. She knew without a trace of doubt that this man was the one true love she had been searching for all her life. She almost swooned when she saw him walking towards her, but she conveniently managed to control herself until he was near enough to catch her in his manly, manly arms.

'My lady,' he said, 'you seem to be suffering from the summer sun. Permit me to assist you.'

'Why, thank you,' Agnes gasped. 'Gosh, you're awfully strong, aren't you?'

'Allow me to introduce myself. I am Captain Cederic Spingly-Spongton of the 3rd Light Dragoons.'

'A captain, you say,' sighed Agnes. 'You must be the son of a very rich and noble lord or something?'

'Alas, I am afraid not, ma'am. My family are but poor farmers from Dorset. But now I have drunk of your beauty, I count myself amongst the richest men in the—'

'Yes, yes, all right,' said Agnes, pushing him away and checking he hadn't ruffled her perfect hair. 'If you don't mind, I have dresses to buy;

I don't have time to stand about talking to paupers. Kindly bog off, you countrified oaf.'

Sheba managed a little smile as she tucked the book back under Gigantus's mattress. The writings of Gertrude Lacygusset had helped a little. For a moment, she even considered letting Gigantus know she had enjoyed it. But then she realised he would probably be furious at her for prying. She had caused more than enough upset already that evening. With a sigh, she began to get ready for bed.

It was only when she took off her cape that she realised something was missing.

She searched every pocket in turn. She found hairpins, Farfellini's pistol, Till's chipped marble – but no sign whatsoever of Mrs Crowley's calling card.

A wave of sick fear slowly spread outwards from her stomach.

She could have dropped it anywhere along the way back from Paradise Street. She could have. But a part of her knew with icy certainty that she hadn't. She had dropped the card in Mrs Crowley's house, behind the door where they had hidden.

She might not find it, Sheba told herself. *She might never go in that room, never think to look behind the door.*

But it was no use trying to convince herself. She had just announced to a murderous villain that she had been spying in her house as clearly as if she had strolled up and left a calling card of her own.

* * *

The Peculiars gathered around the breakfast table the next morning and glumly sipped their coffee. Somewhere in the yard Monkeyboy could be heard waking up. An unpleasant mixture of coughing, hacking, spitting and scratching, followed by the clang of his cage door as he clambered out. Flossy and Raggety were making noises too: whickering and bleating that meant their breakfast oats were long overdue. Sheba would have normally been out to them by now, but today she hadn't the energy.

In the tragedy of losing Matthew, nobody had mentioned what had been discovered at Mrs Crowley's house. The information had cost a great deal, but it was important. Vitally important. Sheba was wondering about the most tactful way to bring it up when Monkeyboy jumped onto the kitchen window sill, making everyone except Sister Moon jump and spill their coffee.

'So,' he said, 'if we've all finished crying about the dead rat, what are we going to do now we know creepy-Crowley is the one what snatched the mudlarks?'

Gigantus looked as if he was going to slap him off the sill and across the yard, but Mama Rat raised a hand to stop him.

'Don't,' she said. 'He doesn't even know what he's saying half the time, let alone how it makes other people feel.' Monkeyboy stared at everyone with a puzzled look, while Mama Rat mopped at the fresh tears leaking from her eyes. After a moment she took a deep breath. 'I suppose he's got a point, though. We need to decide what we do next. I take it you discovered something worthwhile last night?'

'We did,' said Sheba. She put her coffee down, ready to give her account of the night.

Gigantus hurriedly snatched out his pen and journal.

'I'm going to make notes,' he said, bristling, when he realised everyone was staring at him. 'Got a problem with that?'

Sheba began to talk.

Mama Rat nodded and Gigantus scribbled as she told them about the derelict house by the river and the sinister meeting which took place there. As she neared the end, it occurred to her that she could leave out the part about the dropped calling card. Nobody need ever know except her. But that would be a kind of lie: a dishonesty to her friends. She decided they deserved to know, so she confessed that also, even though it was almost in a whisper.

'Not worry,' said Sister Moon. 'Card could fall any place. And even if she find it, Mrs Crowley not know it you. She must give many cards.'

'But if she does turn up here to get us, it's your fault,' said Monkeyboy.

'So, to sum up what we've got,' said Gigantus, ignoring Monkeyboy and reading from his journal, 'Mrs Crowley isn't a grieving mother at all. And she's working with these two weird men for some reason we don't yet know.'

'If it involves an evil painted monster and some kind of doctor, it can't be anything good,' said Mama Rat.

Sheba nodded. 'That doctor, if he even was one, didn't smell like someone who makes people better. He stank of death and rot and evil things.'

'Maybe he chop up bodies,' said Sister Moon. 'Like doctor Large 'Arry talk about.'

'Well, whoever they are,' continued Gigantus, 'they need several children and something important – whatever that is. They got Farfellini to build them a machine, and snatched a bunch of mudlarks that they thought no one would miss. Now all they need to do is get one more child and this thing they want, and they can do . . .' He paused, looking stumped. 'Well, whatever it is they have planned.'

'Well done, Inspector Fatbottom,' said Monkeyboy.

'So many questions still to answer,' added Sister Moon.

'But I don't understand,' said Sheba. 'What could they need the children for?'

'Best not to think about that at the moment, dearie,' said Mama Rat. 'I have a feeling it won't be anything nice. Didn't you say it was tonight's low tide they were going to snatch another mudlark?'

'Yes,' Sheba nodded. 'We need to stop it. And find out where she is keeping the others.'

'They're not in the house,' said Mama Rat. 'While Matthew was . . . was helping you, the others gave the place a quick going over. No sign of any children. Not even in the cellar.'

'But there must be a reason she's taken that tatty house,' said Sheba. 'The place and her just don't fit. I'm sure it's something to do with the river.'

Sister Moon had been standing still for a long while,

frowning in thought. She slowly raised a finger. 'I have idea,' she said. 'A way to stop machine and find children. But I need certain objects—'

Before she could say any more, the front door burst open with a crash.

Everyone leapt out of their seats and rushed into the parlour in time to see the bloated form of Plumpscuttle stagger in from the street. He was never the picture of health when he returned from a night on the town, but now he looked like one of the walking dead. In fact, he looked worse than dead. He looked like the corpse of a warthog, stuffed into the corpse of a hippo, stuffed into a bad suit.

His face was swollen and bruised. Dried blood spattered his torn shirt. One eye was puffed up into a tiny slit. And he appeared to have lost some teeth.

'Set upon!' he cried, collapsing into the battered armchair by the fireplace. 'Set upon by hoodlums and footpads! Someone tried to kill me!'

'Slow down, dearie, and tell us who did this to you.' Mama Rat tried to examine his wounds as he writhed and groaned. He'd clearly been given a serious beating by someone. And it must have been someone pretty big to even make a dent in all the blubber.

'Some thug,' he yelled. 'Some painted, long-haired monster! He caught me on the way to Mrs Crobbin's pie shop and pounded me into pieces! Then he told me to give this to my friends . . . stupid idiot! I don't have any friends!'

Plumpscuttle held something up in his blood-spattered hands, and then passed out with a final groan. As he lay comatose, mouth dribbling blood and gravy, Sister Moon reached down to pry open his fat fingers and remove the tattered thing he had been clutching.

It was a piece of card, now dotted with spots of Plumpscuttle's blood. Even as Moon unfolded it, Sheba knew what it would be.

It was Mrs Crowley's calling card.

Chapter Fourteen

IN WHICH THE PECULIARS GO CRAB FISHING.

Low tide came just after midnight, and had anyone been walking beside the banks of the Thames they would have been treated to a rare sight. A group of oddly-shaped figures, all dressed in black, was apparently about to drown a little urchin dressed in filthy rags and a cloth cap, a length of rope dangling from his waist.

'This idea is utter horse crap!' the urchin shouted.

Gigantus held Monkeyboy in an iron grip. The big man was grinning.

'How far out do you want me to toss him?' he said to

the others. 'I reckon I could send him a good thirty feet at least.'

'If you don't put me down right now, I'm going to do something horrible in your mouth next time you're asleep!' yelled Monkeyboy.

The Peculiars stood at the high-tide line on the south bank, next to an upturned skiff. They had chosen a spot just upriver from Paradise Street, reasoning that Mrs Crowley would be wanting to strike as close to home as possible and to have the crab make its return journey with the current.

Sheba looked around at her friends. The pale faces of Gigantus and Mama Rat bobbed about in the darkness like disembodied turnips. Sister Moon was holding a rusty whaling harpoon that they had discovered in an old iron-monger's on Spicers Street. Attached to it was a whisky bottled filled with white phosphorus, which gave out a dim glow.

A wide stretch of mud lay before them and tonight the surface of the Thames appeared quite beautiful in the light of a full moon, until you looked close enough to see what was floating in it.

'Don't worry,' Sheba said to Monkeyboy. 'There really is no danger. At the first sign of anything bad, Gigantus will haul on the rope and drag you back here to safety. You just have to stand on the mud for a few minutes. You'll be helping. Till and all the mudlarks could be saved because of you.'

'I couldn't give a rat's fart about saving anyone. Now

put me down so I can go back home and have a nice long— aaaaaaaaaaargh!'

Before Monkeyboy could finish his sentence, Gigantus launched him like a human javelin. He flew through the night air, trailing a piteous squeal, and landed with a wet smack right beside the water's edge.

'You didn't have to throw him *quite* so hard, Gigantus,' said Mama Rat.

The little figure struggled to right itself in the smelly slop, then began wailing and trying to wade back to shore.

'Stay there, you putrid little munchkin!' called Gigantus, 'Or I won't bother to pull you back in when whatever-it-is comes for you!'

'You really enjoying this, aren't you?' came Sister Moon's voice from somewhere in the darkness.

'Oh, yes,' said Gigantus happily. 'It was an excellent plan of yours.'

'Well, the trap is set,' said Mama Rat. 'We must take our positions.'

There was a slight rattling of pebbles as Moon stole away. Sheba thought she saw her slip underneath a jetty which jutted out into the river.

When she had outlined her plan in the house that afternoon, it had seemed like a stroke of genius. Out here in the cold night, in the mud, where clawed, child-snatching machines lurked, it seemed like lunacy.

'Good luck, everyone,' Sheba whispered, and saw Gigantus nod as he and Mama Rat ducked behind the old skiff. Then she took a deep breath and set off on her own mission.

At first, everyone had been reluctant to let her go off alone. She was only nine (or possibly ten) and the streets of London weren't a good place for anybody to be on their own, especially a child. However, as she had pointed out, most children didn't carry a pistol full of poisoned darts. *And most children can't turn into snarling, snapping wolfgirls, either.* The voice in her head had added that last bit; she pretended to ignore it.

As she climbed the steps up from the river and started making her way downstream along the Bermondsey Wall, she began to wish she hadn't been so keen. When Sister Moon suggested they would need someone to watch the river between the jetty and Paradise Street, to see if the creature returned there, Sheba volunteered. She did have the best senses of hearing and smell. And besides, the only other alternative was being the decoy. She was quite happy to leave that job to Monkeyboy.

But now it came to walking through the dark streets to Paradise Street all alone, she didn't feel anywhere near as brave. Her stomach flipped at every tiny sound. Underneath the river-stink, scents flooded her nose. Soot and coal dust, gas and the ever-present reek of raw sewage. Her heart pounded in her chest. She could feel her fur bristling and her nose stretching, her teeth growing and her eyes burning orange. Just like when she was angry, fear seemed to bring out the wolf in her.

Sheba slipped through the shadows. She didn't want to stumble into anyone while she looked like this. People might find it amazing when they were paying to see it, but bumping into a snarling wolfgirl down a dark alley was another matter.

Eventually, she came to a set of narrow stone stairs that led down to the river. Directly behind her was Paradise Street. If she was right, Mrs Crowley had needed a place close to the river for a reason. So that Farfellini's machine could get in and out of the mud without being seen.

Half praying she would find the crab machine's hideout, half praying she would never have to set eyes on it, Sheba gritted her little white teeth and set off down the steps, reminding herself as she went: *Be brave, the stolen children need you.*

Somewhere across the river, a church clock chimed. The stakeout on the mudflats had been running for the best part of an hour now.

Out on the mud, the bait had grown tired of flailing, and was now slowly sinking in the septic slop and wailing in a pitiful manner. Gigantus, from his position behind the skiff, had long ceased being amused and was now just cold and tired. Mama Rat was beginning to worry their plan had failed, which meant another victim might have been taken elsewhere on the river.

Crouching beneath the jetty, Sister Moon was the only one still focused. She had entered a trance state of concentration, which she could maintain for several hours. Every ripple and bubble that emerged around the sorry figure of Monkeyboy was noted and processed. The harpoon in her hands was poised, ready for flight.

Lucky for Monkeyboy that one of them was still on the ball, as something was beginning to stir in the silt beneath him. It was almost imperceptible at first; a slight vibration in the jelly-like mud around his legs. Then bubbles began to pop on the surface, followed by a ring of smoking dots . . .

Sister Moon raised the harpoon higher.

With a sudden roar, the mud beneath Monkeyboy collapsed. Red tentacles burst upwards, steam pouring from each one, and a spiked dome heaved itself to the surface. Claws clacked and snapped as they freed themselves from the sticky slime, tearing at Monkeyboy's ragged trousers, and all was lit by the glow from a yellow porthole in the centre. A porthole in which a painted face could be seen, its teeth bared in a fierce grin.

Monkeyboy screamed.

And Moon flung the harpoon, aiming for the thinnest of lines on the creature's back that marked the overlap of its armour plating. Most people wouldn't have been able to see such a tiny detail in the dark, let alone in the space of a heartbeat. The rusty harpoon tip slid into the crab like a dart into butter, and lodged there firmly.

Gigantus, startled into action, heaved on the rope – with a little too much zeal. Monkeyboy shot out of the creature's grasp, and straight into the side of the skiff with a crunching smack.

The creature let out a wail of grinding gears. Within

seconds it had dived back beneath the surface, pulling the harpoon under too. The end jutted out of the mud for a moment, the whisky bottle of phosphorus swinging to and fro before disappearing with the rest. As the ripples of mud slowly subsided, drops of the white substance could be seen glowing in the moonlight.

The crab had been tagged.

Sheba sat at the foot of the narrow stone steps, her feet resting on the slime of the riverbank. She could hear the water lapping at the mud, as the tide crawled slowly in again. The night was drawing to a close, and the river was readying itself for another busy day.

Somewhere on it a steamer chuffed along. Wisps of fog had started blowing past, making ghostly shapes in the moonlight. It was almost as if the wind was trying to entertain her with ever more elaborate swirls and loops. Nothing had the slightest effect on Sheba, however – apart from the smell, which she could hardly avoid. With a handkerchief clamped firmly over her nose, she sat lost in thought.

For the life of her, she couldn't understand what Mrs Crowley could be up to. She must have lured them to the graveyard just to get a look at who was nosing into her business. All that rubbish about her son had been nothing but a pack of lies (the fact Sheba had fallen for it so easily still smarted) but why was she taking so many children? And why only the tatty, half-starved waifs of the riverside?

The painted man seemed to be her servant, but what about the frizzy-haired doctor? She remembered what she had heard in the study in Paradise Street: *We shall have what we most desire. And how long we have waited* . . . What was it they wanted so badly?

The questions wouldn't stop. She thought so hard that her furry little head throbbed. Still, they only had to prove Mrs Crowley had taken the children, and then they could call in the police and let them deal with it. She was just picturing Mrs Crowley being led away in iron handcuffs when her attention was caught by a movement further downriver.

She peered into the darkness. Something was pushing up out of the mud. It was difficult to make out, but it appeared to be big and spiky and slicked with slime. The crab machine! Some kind of rod was jutting out of its back, and it was making a high-pitched keening sound that reminded Sheba of grinding metal. Before she could get a better look, a wave of thicker fog blew across her line of sight.

Sheba cursed. Now the crab could be anywhere, and she was supposed to be following it. She would have to march through the fog, and hope she didn't walk right into it. Taking a deep breath for courage, she began to edge downriver along the bank.

The fog had really set in now, and every step she took sent her deeper into the blankness. She held her breath, ready to run away screaming at the slightest movement. It was difficult to judge exactly where she was going, but by counting her steps she estimated she had gone ten metres or so when she came across a gaping crater in the mud. It was releasing waves of stink so strong that Sheba nearly keeled over backwards. She clamped the handkerchief harder over her nose and peered at the ground.

There were droplets of glowing white liquid on the crater's surface, leading up the bank to a crumbling brick wall and into a rank-smelling tunnel. The entrance was partly hidden by rotten planks of wood, slimy weeds and a rusty grate. It looked (and smelt) just like any other sewer outlet along the riverbank. Sheba would never have spotted it, had it not been for the phosphorus. *That Sister Moon knows a few tricks,* she thought.

Note where the trail leads, and nothing more. That's what Moon had said. But it couldn't hurt if she had a little look. Could it?

Holding her breath, Sheba slipped behind the stack of rotting timber and pulled open the rusty grate. It squealed noisily, and she winced, but there was now enough space for her to squeeze through. The white drops continued up the tunnel; she could see them glowing well into the distance. She took a tentative step into the tunnel mouth, then stopped. The gate swung shut behind her. She couldn't be sure, but it had looked like part of the glowing trail had moved.

Sheba froze. Her heart skipped a beat. There was a scraping sound from further up the shaft, and the drops shifted again. Slowly it came to her: the very furthest spot of light wasn't part of the trail . . . It was like a yellow eye . . . The realisation hit her with a sickening thud. *The crab was still in the tunnel!*

She turned and ran back to the grate. But it was now jammed in place. From behind her, she could hear the sound of something scraping against the stonework, getting louder and closer by the second. The fur on her neck was standing up. She began to growl. There was the chuff of an engine and the hiss of steam and the clank of broken machinery. Her claws were out. She grabbed the grate and pushed with all her strength. She could smell it now: hot oil and smoke, river mud and coal dust. For a terrible moment she thought the grate wasn't going to shift, then suddenly it gave way and she tumbled free of the tunnel mouth, landing on her face in the slimy weeds outside. *I'm safe,* she thought. *All I have to do is get back to the others and tell them where the tunnel is.*

She heaved herself up on all fours, ready to run, when she felt something close around her ankle.

Something cold, hard, serrated . . .

The crab had reached out a claw and grabbed her. With irresistible, mechanical strength, it began to pull her in.

Sheba let out one terrified, growling shriek before she was hauled out of sight and back into the tunnel.

Chapter Fifteen

IN WHICH SHEBA SAMPLES SOME
UNPLEASANT HOSPITALITY.

Sheba was woken by a dim light. At first she thought she was in her bed at Brick Lane, that the night before had been some awful nightmare. Her body soon told her otherwise.

She was frozen to the bone, her dress and cloak clinging in damp, icy folds all over her. Her ankle felt as though it had been run through a mangle. There was a lump on the side of her head that made her head spin every time she moved. Her entire body was stiff and sore. Beneath her she could feel slimy stone. If what had woken her was daylight, then she must have been knocked out cold for the whole night.

With a burst of effort that made flashes appear before her eyes, Sheba pushed herself upright and looked around. Her woozy sight was still adjusting, but she could see she was in some kind of chamber. The daylight came from somewhere to the left. *Must be the tunnel entrance,* she thought. All she could smell was the filthy stink of the river and the rusty scent of hot metal and steam.

She tried to raise a hand to the bump on her head, and briefly panicked when she couldn't. Then she realised her hands had been tied in front of her at the wrist. Coarse rope burnt her furry skin, and her fingertips tingled where the circulation had been cut off. She stretched out her bound hands and touched a series of vertical iron bars.

She was in a cage. Again.

Most people would probably have found this a terrifying discovery, but Sheba had spent most of her life locked away. There was a stone wall behind her; she leant back on it calmly and assessed her situation.

The crab had caught her last night, and its pilot – the painted man, she assumed – had tied her up and thrown her in a cage. She had found the crab's secret hideaway, but the knowledge was useless unless she could tell someone.

Sheba patted her pockets. Whoever had bound her had not thought to search her first. She still had her hairpins and the clockwork pistol. Hopefully it would still work despite the damp. Could she manage to pick the lock with her hands tied? Maybe she could use her claws to scratch through her rope bindings.

A sudden noise beside her made her jump. Peering into the gloom, she found her eyes had adjusted and she could make out vague shapes. There seemed to be more cages. Six or seven at least. In the one next to her, a small, dark bundle was stirring.

'Hello?' she whispered. 'Is anyone there?'

The bundle of rags twitched some more, and then Sheba saw the glint of two large, frightened eyes blinking rapidly.

'Hello?' Sheba tried again. Then she frowned. Was there a familiar scent under the rank stench of river mud? 'Is . . . is that you, Till?'

'Who are you?' The voice that came from the ragged lump was cracked and broken, the voice of someone who hadn't spoken for a long while, but it was enough for Sheba to recognise her friend.

'It's me. Sheba. The girl from the sideshow. The one with . . . with the hair.'

The lump moved some more, growing one spindly white arm then another, and gradually unfolding into the shape of a tiny girl. She shuffled forwards, her bony fingers clutching the iron bars between them.

'Sheba?' The hope in her voice was almost painful to hear. 'But . . . what are you doing here? Did the monster get you?'

Sheba slid over to the bars, ignoring the sudden pain in

her head and ankle. She lifted her bound hands and put them over Till's.

'Till! I'm so glad I've found you! We've been searching and searching for days.'

'You've been searching for me?' Till blinked in surprise. 'But I only met you once. Why would you come looking for a scrap of nothing like me?'

'Because . . . because you were nice to me.' Sheba didn't know how to explain that nobody normal had ever shown kindness to her before. It made her feel embarrassed somehow. Cemented the fact she was so different, so freakish. She tried to change the subject. 'And your parents, they came to us and asked us to help.'

'My parents?' Till's eyes glistened and sparkled in the gloom.

Sheba gave the little girl's fingers a gentle squeeze. 'Yes, they've been looking too. But it's all right now. I've found you. I can tell them where you are.'

'And how are you going to do that, when you're locked in here?' said another voice from further inside the chamber.

Sheba jumped, fearing it might be Mrs Crowley – even though she hadn't smelt her – but whoever it was sounded as tired, weak and terrified as Till.

'There's more of us here,' Till explained. 'Eight others. We all got taken by the monster. We've tried to escape, but there's no way out.'

'There is now,' Sheba said. 'I just have to get these ropes off.'

'It's no good,' said Till. 'The cages are locked. And they comes to check on us all the time. If they think we've been trying to escape, they beat us.'

'Who are *they*?' Sheba asked.

'We call her the Night Lady,' said Till, 'the one what wears black. Her and the big man with the painted face. And sometimes there's another. A man with white hair and spectacles. He doesn't hit us, though. He just prods us and measures us with his devices.'

Sheba absorbed this information. 'Have they said anything to you? Told you why you were taken?'

Till shook her head. 'They don't speak much to us. The Night Lady just laughs when we cry. Then she gets the painted man to hit us. It's better if you don't make a sound.'

'*I've* heard them talking, though,' another voice called out. This one came from the black murk at the far end of the chamber. 'I been here the longest, see. Back when there was just me, I heard them talking together. About something they wanted. A prize, they said. In Hyde Park.'

Sheba recalled the conversation from the Paradise Street house again. *Are you sure you will be able to get it?* the doctor had said. *They have it very well guarded* . . . Whatever they were after was in Hyde Park. She was about to ask what was so special about the place when she remembered Mama Rat's newspaper. The Great Exhibition was in Hyde Park.

Were they going to rob the Crystal Palace? What for? She racked her aching head for what she could remember of the exhibits. The crystal fountain? No, too big. One of the sculptures? Or a machine? None seemed worth all this trouble. Something Mrs Crowley most desired, she had said. What did grown-ups most desire? Money? Fame? Gold? Jewels . . .

'Was it a jewel?' she asked, hesitantly. 'Did the woman mention a diamond?'

There was a moment's silence from the cages, then one of the voices spoke.

'She might have,' it said.

'I think she did,' called another.

The Koh-i-Noor. That had to be it. Mrs Crowley was after the world's biggest diamond. Maybe she was going to make the children steal it.

'We have to get out of here,' Sheba whispered to Till.

'But I told you,' Till whispered back. 'There's no way out. The cages are locked.'

'Not for long,' said Sheba. She began to wriggle and turn her wrists, ignoring the burning and chafing, trying to loosen the rope so she could get her hands free. In her panic, she could feel the wolf inside her growing. But instead of suppressing it, she let it in, welcoming the extra surge of strength and ferocity it gave her.

The rope ripped hair from her arms and blistered her skin, but she kept pulling and pulling. Eventually she felt it begin to loosen a little. A bit more and she could squeeze a hand free.

A booming clang echoed from somewhere beyond the chamber. It was followed by voices, distant at first, but growing rapidly closer.

'They're coming!' Till hissed, dashing to the back of her cage. 'Sheba, they're coming!'

There was the shrill sound of squeaking hinges, and the grating of ancient wood on stone. Somewhere a door was being opened. Sheba strained to see, and was instantly blinded by a flare of searing light. Falling backwards, hands pressed over her face, she thought there had been some kind of silent explosion, but as she peered through her fingers she could see it was only the light from a lantern.

There were three figures. Without much surprise, she recognised Mrs Crowley, the painted man she had called Baba Anish and the frizzy-haired doctor. She could smell the doctor's twisted medical stink, and the pungent incense of the other. A cruel, curved sword hung at his side, and he had freshly painted his face with glistening black whorls. His eyes were rimmed with black and his long, matted locks were coiled on the top of his head in a swirling bundle. He looked even more hostile than when Sheba had last seen him. Perhaps he was angry that they had speared his machine.

She also noticed the dark passageway they had stepped from. Where did it lead? Back to Paradise Street? *I knew there was a reason for her staying there.* The fact she had been right didn't give Sheba much satisfaction now.

Mrs Crowley paused to light a torch on the wall. Now Sheba could see they were indeed in a large chamber made of heavy stone. Ribbed arches supported the roof. They looked ancient, crumbling. A row of cages stretched around the wall, each one holding the small, shivering body of a child. To her left was what had to be the tunnel entrance, glowing dimly. Down there, just the length of a short dash, were the river, her friends and freedom. But it might as well have been a hundred miles away.

Right in front of the cages was a wide pit. Steps led down to a muddy bottom, where the mechanical crab sat in a mud-spattered pile. Hooked chains on pulleys dangled over it. Sheba could clearly see Sister Moon's whaling harpoon jutting out of the crab's back. She had thrown it perfectly: its barbed tip had sunk straight into the machinery inside. Even now smoke was slowly leaking from the machine while thick oil poured out to pool around it like clotting blood. It looked dead, if that could be true of something that had never really lived. It was broken, at any rate. If Sheba hadn't achieved anything else, at least it wouldn't be snatching any more mudlarks from the river.

'A harpoon? I don't believe it,' Mrs Crowley said. Her lisping voice echoed around the stone room, making Sheba jump. 'Has the thing been badly damaged?'

'I can't get it to work any more,' said Baba Anish. 'And without the puppet man—'

'Those interfering freaks!' Mrs Crowley slammed her lantern down on the floor, cracking the glass. It was the first time Sheba had seen a dent in her cool exterior. 'I thought you said you'd warned them off? Didn't you beat their leader hard enough?'

The painted man shrugged. Sheba wondered who they

meant by 'leader'. Then she realised it was Plumpscuttle. If she hadn't been so scared out of her wits, she might have laughed.

'Where is the one you captured?'

Baba Anish pointed to Sheba's cage.

Mrs Crowley walking towards her was like a shadow peeling itself from the wall and becoming solid. Under the featureless veil, Sheba imagined a face twisted in rage. But instead of cowering back, Sheba rose on her knees, snarling and showing her white little fangs. She could smell the chemical odour of the woman quite strongly now, and beneath it that familiar odour she couldn't quite place. A flower of some kind? A perfume? It was definitely something she had smelt before. But where?

The veiled woman paused outside the cage, and seemed to be staring at her again, just like she had in the graveyard. It was a different kind of stare to the ones Sheba usually received. More intense. She could almost feel the woman thinking as the seconds of silence ticked by.

She's probably deciding on the best place to kick me, Sheba thought. But when Mrs Crowley spoke, her voice was calm. She sounded almost amused.

'It's the little girl, is it? The rat woman's "daughter", if that is to be believed. Were you the one snooping around my house, or was it one of your . . . *malformed* friends?' The woman almost spat the word, making Sheba wince.

'It was me,' said Sheba. Let her take whatever punishment this horrid woman would give, if it meant the others would be left alone.

'On your own? I hardly think so. I suppose you expect me to believe you threw the harpoon that ruined my machine as well?'

'No, but I followed the trail.'

Mrs Crowley looked again at the crab. The bottle hanging from the harpoon end still trickled drops of phosphorus onto the rusty carapace.

'Very ingenious,' said Mrs Crowley. 'But for all your cunning, it only got you as far as this cage. I would call that a failure, wouldn't you?'

'I know what you're planning,' Sheba said. 'That's not a failure.' It probably wasn't the best thing to blurt out, but the woman was making Sheba angry. Even as she spoke she could feel her snout jutting out and her ears tweaking into points.

Mrs Crowley gave a tinkling laugh. 'Come on, then. Let's hear it.'

'You're going to steal the Koh-i-Noor from the Great Exhibition!' Sheba shouted. 'You're going to make the children take it, so they get the blame!'

She half expected Mrs Crowley to scream in frustration. Instead, the woman turned her shrouded face to where the two men stood. The three looked at each other for a few seconds, and then the doctor and Mrs Crowley burst out laughing. Even Baba Anish allowed himself a smirk.

Sheba was left speechless. What was so funny? Had she got it wrong?

'I suppose there's a hint of truth there,' Mrs Crowley said, when she had stopped chuckling. 'It would be nice to see the look on your face when you realise how close you came. Pity that won't be possible, what with you being *dead*. Unless you think we can use her, Doctor?'

The bald man shuffled over to her cage and peered at her through his spectacles, which were so thick that his eyes seemed to swim behind them, like two blue goldfish in their bowls. One of his gangly hands shot through the bars and grabbed the crown of her head. Sheba could feel his fingers squeezing and prodding at her skull.

'No, I'm afraid the material would be too tainted,' he said, at last. 'It might hinder the properties of the formula.'

Formula? What was the man talking about? And what did her head have to do with it? Sheba was frantically trying to make sense of what was going on.

'Curse it,' said Mrs Crowley. Her lisp had almost turned to a hiss in her anger. 'We shall have to hope what we've already got will be enough. We have no time to collect any more: everything is in place for tonight. I have even arranged for several of the guards to be elsewhere. You had best start moving the children.'

The doctor nodded and went to fetch a ring of heavy iron keys from the wall. Sheba heard herself snarling and growling in frustration. She had only just found the children and now they were moving them somewhere else. But where? And how?

'Baba Anish,' Mrs Crowley called. 'These sideshow

freaks are obviously more trouble than we anticipated. Fetch those murderous thugs you have been recruiting, and pay them a visit. I want them all dead before tonight's proceedings, just in case they try to get in the way.'

'No!' screamed Sheba. The thought of her friends being harmed made her fling herself at the cage bars over and over. 'Leave them alone, you evil witch! Leave them alone!'

'And as for this one,' Mrs Crowley paused on her way out of the chamber. She seemed to be considering something. Finally she shook her head, pressed a hand to her brow. 'Stake her out in the tunnel. The tide is coming in. It should make short work of her.'

'Yes, *memsahib*,' said Baba Anish. He moved towards Sheba's cage, the black patterns on his face seeming to move like snakes in the lantern's light.

'Oh, and Anish?' Mrs Crowley called back from the door. 'Be careful. She bites.'

Chapter Sixteen

When Baba Anish first tied her to the iron stakes he had hammered into the tunnel floor, Sheba thought she might be able to pull them out after he had gone. The ground was only river mud and pebbles, after all.

She soon found she was wrong. The stakes were long – long enough to reach through the soft mud and bite into something harder and less yielding. She tried heaving at each of the pegs that held her arms and legs in turn, but to no effect. Not even when she got scared and felt the usual surge of wolfish strength. They wouldn't budge.

Next she tried screaming. The river wasn't far away – she could hear it. Someone must be passing the tunnel. Surely they would hear her and come to investigate?

Sheba yelled until her throat was raw.

Nobody came.

So now she lay on her back, looking up at the slimy brickwork above her. Water was steadily filling the tunnel now. She could feel it seeping under her legs. Maybe only a few centimetres at the moment, but rising rapidly. It looked as though she was going to meet her end here, slowly covered by the stinking Thames water, while a few miles away her friends were chopped into pieces by Baba Anish and his Ratcliff Highway friends.

The bodies of Plumpscuttle's Peculiars might be found – they'd probably get a mention in the newspaper – but she would lie forever in this damp and lonely tunnel. Maybe in two hundred years or so someone would find her bones and wonder why a little girl had been tied down and left for the eels to eat.

She was quietly thinking morbid thoughts to herself, letting her tears trickle down to join the pool of water beneath her, when she felt something move by her foot. The eels had come to eat her already! Sheba shrieked and tried to jerk her leg away, but couldn't. She raised her head, hardly daring to look, and expected to see a slimy head with a mouthful of needle-sharp teeth and blank eyes.

Instead, there was a huge black rat sitting on her shoe.

Its fur glistened with river slime and its beady eyes sparkled in the half-light of the tunnel. She hadn't even thought about the rats. The riverside must be thick with them, and they wouldn't bother waiting for her to die before they began feasting. Being eaten alive by rats would *really* hurt.

'Go away,' Sheba tried to shout. But it came out of her hoarse throat as a pathetic croak.

The rat gave several loud, piercing squeaks – and more rats scuttled down from the tunnel mouth. Soon there were five of them perched on Sheba's legs. The end had come, then, and there was nothing she could do. But just before she squeezed her eyes shut, preparing herself for the first nibble, she saw the first rat do something extra- ordinary: it put its little paws on its hips and rolled its eyes. Sheba even thought she heard it make something that sounded like a 'tut'. She felt a tiny flicker of hope.

'Bartholomew?' she said, slowly. 'Judas, Thaddeus, Simon and Peter?'

The rats squeaked and chattered. Sheba had never thought she'd be so glad to see a pack of rodents.

'Do you think you could get me out of here?' she asked. 'The others are in danger. I have to get back to them!'

The rats instantly dashed to the ropes at her arms and legs and began gnawing. Sheba lay very still as their yellow teeth chewed and chomped. After a few minutes, she felt her left leg spring free. It wasn't long before the other leg followed, then her hands. She sat up, rubbing at the burnt skin around her wrists, while the rats clustered around, looking up at her with their bright little eyes.

'Thank you so much,' said Sheba. 'That's twice you've saved my life now.' If they weren't quite so slime-covered and generally revolting, she could have kissed them. Instead she gave them what she hoped was a grateful smile.

'I have to get to Brick Lane,' she said. 'I don't suppose you can show me the quickest way?'

The rats instantly scampered off down the tunnel, waiting for Sheba at the entrance. With a groan, she forced herself to stand and began to stagger after them. Her bruised body wanted nothing more than to curl up and sleep, preferably after a warm bath and change of clothes, but she had to warn the others before Baba Anish came for them.

As she limped out of the tunnel that had so nearly become her tomb, she prayed she would be in time.

Back at Brick Lane, the Peculiars were sitting morosely in the yard, when there came a frantic hammering at the gate. Sister Moon opened it a fraction, blade at the ready, and saw a furry, shaggy blob of mud with frantic orange eyes and a cluster of rats at its feet. It took her a moment to recognise Sheba.

'You're alive!' Moon shouted, pulling her into the yard and hugging her tightly, despite her coating of stinking mud. 'Sheba, we so worried!'

The rest of the Peculiars jumped up and clustered

around, cheering and clapping. The rats dashed up to Mama.

'Well done, my boys! My clever beauties!' she cried.

'There's no time!' Sheba shouted, pushing Sister Moon away. 'Mrs Crowley's servant is coming here right now! He's coming to kill us!'

'But what happened to you?' Gigantus asked, his craggy face creased with worry. 'Where have you been?'

As fast as she was able, Sheba blurted out everything that had happened to her: following the crab machine's trail, being caught, finding the mudlarks, discovering Mrs Crowley's plan and finally being staked out in the tunnel. She barely paused for breath. 'And Baba Anish is coming here to get you, now.'

'Well, we've seen no sign of him,' said Gigantus. 'And he doesn't stand much chance against all of us on his own.'

'He's hiring some thugs,' Sheba remembered. 'He'll probably be here any minute.'

'Right, that's it . . . I'm off,' said Monkeyboy. He made to run for the yard gate, but Gigantus caught hold of his tail.

'None of us is going anywhere,' the big man said. 'At least not until tonight, when we go and put a stop to this woman's plans once and for all. If this makeup-wearing idiot wants a fight, then he can bring it on.'

'But he's going to kill you!' Sheba wanted to give Gigantus a shake, but knew it would be like a flea trying to budge a mountain.

'Maybe we should leave,' said Mama Rat. 'We could use the time to get to Hyde Park and stop Crowley in the act.'

'That sounds like a brilliant idea,' said Monkeyboy.

Sister Moon agreed, and to Sheba's relief Gigantus reluctantly nodded. They all headed back into the house to grab what they might need.

Just as they were making their final preparations, a hideous groan came from the front room. Plumpscuttle. He was finally coming round.

The Peculiars poked their head round the door of the parlour.

'Is he dying?' Monkeyboy whispered, hopefully.

Plumpscuttle groaned loudly and tried to sit up, then quickly lay back down again. He looked as though an entire tonne of fireworks had just gone off in his head. His piggy eyes seemed to bulge in time to his heartbeat. Underneath the dried blood and gravy stains, his skin was white and clammy. He tried to speak, but all that came out was 'Whyaaaaaaaaaaaargh?' The effort made him pass out again.

'What's wrong with him?' Gigantus asked. He didn't sound very sympathetic.

'It looks like he's concussed,' said Mama Rat. 'Maybe he could be hurt elsewhere too. A broken rib or something. That Baba Anish chappie did a good job on him.'

'About time someone did,' Gigantus said. He looked as though he wished it had been him.

'I think we ought to take him to hospital, you know.' Mama Rat was holding one of his fat wrists, checking his pulse. 'He should be looked at by a doctor. And besides, we can't just leave him here if a bunch of cut-throats are about to come calling.'

'Why not?' said Monkeyboy. 'They can finish the job properly this time.'

Everyone chose to ignore him.

'The London Hospital near,' Sister Moon suggested. 'Gigantus take him and meet us back here?'

Sheba was about to object, but Gigantus was already reaching to pick him up.

'Don't worry, Sheba,' said Gigantus. 'I'm just dumping him off. I'll be back before you know it.'

The minutes that Gigantus was missing seemed to crawl past like hours. Sheba paced the floorboards of the front room, while the others stood about, fidgeting nervously. *This is a mistake*, she thought. *We should have gone while we had the chance.* But if they had left Plumpscuttle here, then he would surely have been killed in their place. He was a horrid, gluttonous blob, but did he really deserve that? *Of course he doesn't*, Sheba told herself. *Nobody does, not even a human dumpling who treats us like cattle.*

'Hurry up, hurry up,' she muttered under her breath.

'I'm sure he's going as fast as he can, dearie,' said Mama Rat.

Sheba was about to say it wasn't fast enough, when there came a splintering bang from the front door.

'It's Baba Anish!' she cried. 'He's here! I knew this would happen . . . what are we going to do without Gigantus?'

'We can manage without him, dearie,' said Mama Rat. 'I've been in tighter scrapes than this before.'

'Quick,' said Sister Moon. 'Upstairs.'

Sheba ran up the stairs as fast as her little feet would go. Sister Moon, Mama Rat and the rats were close behind. Monkeyboy seemed to have dashed into the kitchen. They burst into the bedroom, ran across to the window and looked out into the yard.

A hulking, bald man in a blood-spattered apron was trying to slip through the gate silently. Sheba recognised him as one of the goons Baba Anish had been talking to at the tavern. But where was the painted man himself?

The enormous cleaver the butcher was carrying had a strange effect on Raggety and Flossy. The big horse began to make a low sound like a growling tiger, and Flossy actually leapt right out of the stall and butted the intruder with both of his little heads.

'Flossy, no!' Sheba called, but her voice was lost in the sound of his manic bleating.

The butcher, after a moment's shock at seeing a sheep with two heads, began to swing his cleaver at the little lamb.

Sheba screwed her eyes shut and turned away, listening for the hideous sound of Flossy being cleaved into chops. It didn't come. Instead she heard the creak of the kitchen window opening. The butcher was so intent on killing Flossy that he missed seeing Monkeyboy somersault through the open window and drop down, unnoticed, into Raggety's stall.

Sheba opened her eyes again to see Monkeyboy quietly unbolt the stall door and clamber onto Raggety's back. If the butcher looked up and saw him now, there would be monkey sausages on the menu, as well as lamb chops.

Raggety found the autumn months very dull, and spent most of the time idly chewing straw and turning his nose up at the cloying smoke and fog. Now his gate was open. Any chance to get out of his stall and stretch his massive legs was welcome, and if he got to assault someone in the process, so much the better.

The butcher had just taken a mighty swipe at Flossy, missing him completely, and was readying himself to kick the little lamb across the yard. His expression quickly changed to one of horror as he got a close view of a very big horse raising its very big hind legs for the mother of all kicks.

Before he could blink, Raggety smashed both hooves into his chest. The blow sent the butcher clear off his feet, across the yard and through the door of the little privy. It was not the sturdiest of buildings. The butcher crashed straight through the seat and into the cesspit below. There was a cry of pain, followed by another of utter disgust and then silence.

'Well done, Raggety!' shouted Sheba from the bedroom window.

'Yes! You beauty!' cried Monkeyboy, and he slapped Raggety on the rump.

This was a mistake.

The horse had seen the tempting street beyond the

open gate. He knew that through there somewhere were lanes and pastures full of sweet clover, just like the ones he visited in the summer. In a split second he was through the gate and off, with Monkeyboy clinging to his back and screaming, 'Not that way, you mangy nag! Turn around! Turn around!'

As the sound of Monkeyboy's screaming faded, the front door reverberated with another mighty bang. Baba Anish? Or another of his thugs? There was no telling how many were on their way to Brick Lane.

Quickly, Sheba scurried to the top of the stairs, looking down to the parlour below. Mama Rat moved to the empty rat's box, flicking open a secret panel in the bottom of it. She drew out her long-barrelled flintlock. Seeing this reminded Sheba of Farfellini's pistol, and she fished it from the pocket of her sodden cloak. She checked it to make sure it was wound and not too damp, then glanced over her shoulder to see Sister Moon drawing her two slim swords. The look on her face was cold and deadly. They all held their breath as they heard the door squeak open.

Then there was a pause. Time seemed to stand very still. Sheba imagined someone very large and very violent standing just outside, preparing to charge in.

Which was exactly what happened next.

The other goon from the tavern, the one with a black bushy beard, stormed through, roaring a battle cry and waving a wooden club. He took the stairs three at a time, bellowing all the way — right into the path of Sheba's pistol. There was a small *twang* as she fired. The little dart hit him square between the eyes. He stopped. *Thank goodness it still works*, thought Sheba. The man stood swaying on the stairs for a moment. Then the flesh of his face began to bubble like a pot of pea soup as scores of boils began to erupt all over his skin. Within seconds, his whole body was covered with fat, angry spots. They even peeped out of his thick, fuzzy beard. Wailing like a girl, he tumbled back down the stairs then struggled to his feet and sprinted out of the front door and down the road.

'Good shooting, Sheba,' said Sister Moon, behind her.

Sheba was just about to allow herself to feel relieved, then she saw something that rendered her dumb. Stepping through the doorway, curved sword drawn, was Baba Anish.

He turned his slow gaze up the stairs, catching sight of Sheba where she crouched on the top step. His face twisted in surprise for a moment, before returning to its normal expression. That of someone about to kill you and everyone you cared about.

Sheba sprang back out of sight but it was too late.

'I see you escaped the tunnel, *memsahib*,' he called as he walked slowly up the stairs.

Thud. Thud.

'Impressive. But you really are a stupid girl.'

Thud. Thud.

'You should have used your freedom to get as far away from this house as possible. Everyone in it is about to die most horribly. My goddess Kali will soon be drinking blood from your empty skulls.'

Thud. Thud.

Sheba looked in desperation to Sister Moon. The ninja reached into one of the pouches at her belt and pulled out a little cloth bag, which she threw to Sheba. Inside were metal ball bearings. *What am I supposed to do with these?* she thought. *Challenge him to a game of marbles and hope he forgets about killing us?*

Sister Moon mimed tipping the bag, before raising her swords again and moving into a complicated-looking stance with the grace of a ballerina. One blade was raised above her head, the other levelled at groin height. Her legs were bent, poised and ready to spring.

Thud. Thud.

Sheba emptied the entire contents of the bag down the steps.

There was a sudden scrambling sound, followed by a loud curse and a series of thumps. She peered over the banister to see Baba Anish land in a crumpled heap at the bottom. She was about to suggest everyone used the few seconds she had bought to make an escape through the bedroom window when she caught a truly repulsive scent.

Stomping in from the kitchen was the butcher. Somehow he had managed to climb out of the privy-hole.

Sheba watched, helpless with horror, as Baba Anish got to his feet and the pair of them started up the stairs, the butcher leading. He seemed to have lost his cleaver in the privy-hole, but his fists looked dangerous enough.

Sheba raised her shaky hands and fired her pistol again. But her nerves spoilt her aim this time, and the dart thudded into the wall, just past the butcher's shoulder. She frantically tried to wind the pistol for another shot. There was a twang and a crunch as a cog jammed. The gun was now useless.

Throwing it to one side, she felt fear and anger rippling under her skin. Her body responded to the adrenalin and stretched itself into a new, more deadly shape. Her sharp teeth gnashed, her claws itched to scratch and slash, and this time it didn't worry her. She wanted to rip these people who had invaded her home and threatened her friends into pieces.

With a snarling scream, she ran headlong at the butcher.

The last thing she remembered was the smell of human waste as the man's fist swung towards her. She was smacked clear across the bedroom, hit the far wall and slid to the bottom in a heap.

Fat lot of use I was, she thought. She watched the rest of the attack in fuzzy, slow motion – almost as if she were having a bad dream.

Far from being futile, Sheba's act had distracted the butcher for an instant, allowing Mama Rat to step up. She pointed her own pistol at the man's head, but before she could shoot, her rats shot out from the pockets of her coat and swarmed up his body and onto his face. In a frenzy of scratching claws and nipping teeth they began to shred his nose. Howling in pain and terror, and trying to grab at the writhing, slippery rodents, he turned and pounded down the stairs past Baba Anish, and out of the house.

The painted man wasn't fazed for an instant. Mama Rat levelled her pistol at his face as he reached the top of the stairs, but wasn't quick enough. Baba Anish moved with frightening speed, reaching to his belt and lunging in one motion. A throwing knife flipped through the air, too fast for Sister Moon to intercept, and thudded into Mama Rat's shoulder.

Sheba and Sister Moon cried out as the woman and her pistol clattered to the floor.

Baba Anish stepped calmly into the bedroom, raising his curved sword and smiling.

Moon's usual calm evaporated. With a furious cry, she launched herself at the intruder, and they began to fight.

It was like a frenzied and incredibly dangerous dance. The weapons of the two moved so fast, it was impossible for Sheba to follow. Both combatants were surrounded by shimmering arcs of steel flashes, and the sound of metal on metal beat out a staccato rhythm, like a madman with a set of teaspoons.

Moon seemed to have the advantage at first. Her sheer anger forced Baba Anish back a step, then another as he fended blow after blow. But before long she began to tire. Her immaculate swordplay faltered. The painted man parried a downward cut, then flipped his sword around, reversing his grip and jabbing upwards. The blade nicked Moon's left forearm, sending a tiny splatter of blood across her cheek. She jumped back from the stairwell, gasping. It was the first time anyone had managed to land a strike on her.

Baba Anish laughed at her shocked expression.

'I am going to gut you,' he whispered, 'then send the hairy girl and the woman to my mistress, Kali. She will enjoy feasting on their souls.'

'Not if I have anything to do with it,' came a low and deeply furious voice from the front door.

It was Gigantus.

Sheba would have cheered if she had been able to move her mouth.

Baba Anish spun to meet the new threat, and happened to meet Gigantus's right fist, which was travelling towards his face at about a hundred miles an hour. It slammed into his mouth with a tooth-shattering crunch, accompanied by the sound of his jaw breaking in several places at once. He staggered back into the room, past the prone bodies of Mama Rat and Sheba, then Gigantus grabbed him by the collar and threw him through the bedroom window and out into the yard. He left a brief, shining arc of smashed glass and blood behind him, and then landed on the packed mud with a solid thump.

Gigantus and Moon stood panting for a moment, looking at each other and the shattered mess around them. They were too tired for words, too tired to do anything but stare, until Mama Rat groaned and they both rushed to her side.

Chapter Seventeen

IN WHICH THE PECULIARS VISIT
THE GREAT EXHIBITION.

'Hold still.'

Sister Moon was trying to sew up the wound in Mama Rat's shoulder. Baba Anish's knife had cut deep, but luckily only into the muscle. Mama sat with her teeth gritted and her face pale. Sheba held her hand.

'Did anyone see where the little idiot went?' Gigantus asked. He was downstairs by the broken front door, looking up and down the street for Monkeyboy. When nobody answered he shut the door, then tutted as it swung open again. 'We're going to need a new lock.'

'And new window,' said Sister Moon. 'Plumpscuttle go mad.'

'Let's hope he stays in hospital for a while, then,' muttered Gigantus.

Sheba looked around the battered house. There was blood and broken glass all over the floor. The wall by the stairs had huge chunks and slices chopped out of it by Sister Moon and Baba Anish. *Baba Anish* . . .

Still feeling shaky, she got to her feet and tottered to the smashed window. Being careful to avoid the broken glass around the edges, she looked down into the yard. There was nothing there. He was gone.

She dashed down the stairs, calling to Gigantus, and ran into the yard. There was a large bloodstained spatter, where he must have landed, dotted with the twinkle of glass shards. Smaller puddles of red led through the open side gate, where they soon mingled with the muck and cobbles of Brick Lane, trampled into smudges by the crowds.

'I shouldn't worry,' said Gigantus from behind her. 'I don't expect he'll last long after what we did to him. Someone'll find his body on the street somewhere.'

Sheba hoped someone *would* find him. Find him and chuck him into the river for the eels to eat, just like he'd tried to do to her. But even as Gigantus shut and bolted the gate, she couldn't help feeling that they hadn't seen the last of him.

* * *

It was a few hours before Monkeyboy turned up. By then Mama Rat was properly bandaged and drinking tea, while Sheba had calmed Flossy down after his ordeal with the butcher, soaked in a hot bath and put on some clean clothes. Her whole body was a mass of bruises and scrapes, and she felt as though she could sleep for a week. She was just telling the others what had happened to her in the tunnel again, when there was a pounding at the door.

With the handle still broken, it swung wide to reveal a group of angry-looking costermongers. They were leading a huge, grumpy Shire horse, with a fuming Monkeyboy on its back.

'Is this your blooming 'orse?' one said. He looked as though he wanted to thump someone. At least until Gigantus stood up and stomped over to the door.

'Yes,' said Gigantus. 'What of it?'

'Oh, nothing, sir.' The costermonger took off his hat and cowered. 'We just thought you'd like 'im back.'

Gigantus took the reins, while the men hurried back along Brick Lane.

Monkeyboy called after them. 'I told you my friend was bigger than you!'

'Watch who you're calling friend, imp,' said Gigantus. But Sheba could tell he was secretly relieved to see Monkeyboy was back safe and sound.

It turned out that Raggety had galloped straight to the nearest market and eaten almost an entire stall of flowers before the men had managed to drag him away. They would have called the police, had one of them not recognised Monkeyboy from Plumpscuttle's sideshow.

'They said they were going to give me a good hiding,' he said, once Sheba had coaxed Raggety back in his stall with more sugar. 'So I told them I hadn't changed my undercrackers in six months.'

'What now, then?' Mama Rat asked.

There was a long, silent pause as everyone considered their options.

'We know she's going to rob the Great Exhibition tonight,' said Sheba. 'Maybe we could tell the police, get them to arrest her?'

Gigantus shook his craggy head. 'No policeman in his right mind is going to believe a story like that. Especially when it comes from a bunch of weirdos like us.'

'I know,' said Monkeyboy. 'How about we just forget the whole thing? It was fun while it lasted, but nearly being killed more than once in a day is just being greedy.'

Mama Rat pretended she hadn't heard him. 'Well, we don't know where this doctor has taken the children – or why he wants them. But it's bound to be something horrid. The only lead we have is the Exhibition. You did say you wanted to see it, Sheba.'

Sheba nodded, remembering how exotic it had sounded when she read about it in the paper. But that was before she knew she'd have to try and break into the place and thwart an evil mastermind.

The hansom cab screeched to a halt at Hyde Park Corner. Sparks had been flying from the left axle all the way from

Whitechapel, where Gigantus's weight had been forcing the suspension down onto bare metal. As its strange cargo poured out of the door, the cab sprang back upright with such force that the cabbie nearly shot off his perch at the front.

'That's two shillings!' he shouted. 'Not including the damage you've done to me blooming axle!'

One of the passengers flung a handful of copper pennies up at him, as the odd group ran off toward Hyde Park.

'Oi! This isn't enough!' the cabbie yelled after them, but the Peculiars were already out of earshot.

'This way,' Gigantus panted as he ran. 'It's before midnight, so the gates are still open, even if the Exhibition is closed.'

There were several small groups of people walking in and out of the park. At the sight of the huge man charging towards them like a bull elephant, surrounded by shadowy figures in black, they scattered in all directions.

As Sheba ran alongside the others, she gaped at the architecture around her. To the left was a huge stone block of a mansion, with a massive portico jutting out of the front. Next to it was an immense gateway: three stone arches big enough to drive a carriage through, and rows of stone columns in between. In fact, there were so many columns about, Sheba thought for a moment the cab might have taken her to Ancient Greece by mistake.

'That's the Duke of Welly's house,' said Monkeyboy, as they passed the mansion. 'Shall we give him a knock?

I bet he'd be up for helping us out.'

'Where's the Exhibition?' asked Sheba. She'd been expecting an enormous glass palace filling the horizon: spires jutting skyward and glinting in the starlight. All she could see now were trees and bushes.

'This way,' said Gigantus. 'Down Rotten Row.' He pointed to a long, straight, sandy track that ran into the park. It was lined with trees and benches, most occupied by huddles of ragged women and children.

The Peculiars set off down the track at a jog. Sheba was impatient to get to the Crystal Palace as quickly as possible, but Mama Rat was already breathing hard. Sister Moon and Monkeyboy loped easily beside her, and from the bushes nearby she could hear rustling and scurrying that could only be the rats. Her own legs were beginning to ache when they came to a little bridge.

'We get off road now,' said Sister Moon. 'There are soldiers.'

Up ahead a small patrol was marching behind their sergeant. All had long rifles with bayonets fixed to the ends. The Peculiars quickly scurried behind the nearest bush.

'You think that's bad,' whispered Gigantus. 'There's a whole flipping barracks full of them just over the road.'

But Sheba didn't really hear him. She was looking past the soldiers, to where a wide, clear river stretched off into the park. The stars were reflected in its clear surface. Compared to the chaos of the Thames, it looked so peaceful and serene.

'Holy pigeon turds on toast,' said Monkeyboy, who was crouching next to her.

'I know,' said Sheba. 'Beautiful, isn't it.'

'Not the Serpentine, you plum! *That*!'

When Sheba saw what he meant, her mouth fell open in sheer awe.

It wasn't the fairytale palace she had imagined. It was far more spectacular than that.

There were no turrets or towers or drawbridges, just a jaw-droppingly amazing man-made structure. A vast, almost endless construction of glass and metal. In the centre were tiers, like the biggest wedding cake in the universe, topped with a huge curved arch. And it was entirely made of ironwork and glass. So much glass. If they'd taken every pane from every single house and building in London, it still wouldn't have been enough. Sheba didn't understand how it didn't collapse under its own weight. The sheer size, the mechanics, of such a thing made her head begin to spin. How had they done it? How was it even imagined?

'It's . . . it's . . .' she tried to say, but words failed her.

'The biggest greenhouse in the world?' said Monkeyboy.

The Peculiars stared as the glow of gas lamps and moonlight played across the vast expanses of shining glass before them. It was so magnificent, they all forgot for a moment why they were there.

'Well, how are we going to get in?' Monkeyboy said at last. 'We can't fly up to the roof, and if we try and smash in through the wall, we'll be full of lead before we can blink.'

From where they hid they could see more patrols of guards and policemen wandering around. There were also two large police lodges between the palace and the park's edge.

'That's an entrance, there,' said Gigantus, pointing to a series of doors at the east end of the building, which was closest to the Peculiars. But the doors looked securely locked, and a policeman was standing sentry.

'If we get to back wall, I can cut way in,' said Sister Moon.

'What we need is a diversion,' said Sheba.

There was a brief silence, in which all eyes turned to Monkeyboy.

'Oh no,' he said. 'Don't even look at me. I've been used as bait once already. It's someone else's turn now.'

'Maybe one of us could run down to the far end,' said Sheba. 'Throw a stone through the glass, draw the soldiers' attention . . . wait a minute! What are they doing?'

The five rats had scurried out of the bush and were dashing towards one of the police lodges.

'Come back!' Mama Rat hissed after them.

'I think,' said Sheba, 'that they're giving us our diversion.'

The little cluster of black shadows disappeared into the lodge. Everyone held their breath and Sheba felt Mama Rat squeezing her arm. Moments later, there was a piercing scream and the sound of a gunshot.

Within seconds there were soldiers and policemen from all over the park, running towards the source of the noise.

'Now!' hissed Sheba. 'Quickly!'

As fast as they could, the Peculiars sprinted across the grass to the rear of the Crystal Palace, just around the corner from the east entrance. Sister Moon had already drawn something from her belt. It looked like two small sticks joined by a piece of string.

Working quickly, she slapped one of the sticks on to the wall. A ball of sticky rubber held it in place. Next, she stretched out the string, and then pressed the other stick against the glass. Using the stuck piece as an anchor, she dragged the second stick around in a wide circle, and then pulled. A perfectly round section of glass popped out from the wall with a slight grinding sound.

'Diamond cutter,' she said, smiling. 'To save diamond. Now in, quickly!'

Not needing to be told twice, the Peculiars clambered through, emerging into a dark, silent room. After Gigantus had squeezed his bulk in, Sister Moon rested the glass back against the wall. Hopefully no one would spot the hole.

'Well, we're in,' said Gigantus. 'Where's this stupid diamond, then?'

'I think,' said Sheba, casting her mind back to the articles she had read back in that other, far more boring life, 'that it's in the centre. Next to the big fountain.'

The Peculiars took a moment to look around. In the darkness, it seemed as though the room was full of hulking metal monsters with jutting spikes and blades. They were all reminded of the mechanical crab, and Gigantus looked ready to pound the nearest one into scrap – just in case it might be used for snatching children.

'Farm machines,' said Sister Moon, using her night sight to read a plaque. 'From America.'

They were about to head towards the door of the room when something scrabbled at the glass behind them.

They turned as one, expecting to see a squad of soldiers with rifles levelled straight at them.

Instead, a writhing bundle of black fur heaved its way up and through the hole they had cut. It separated into five squeaking rats.

Mama Rat bent down to cuddle them all with a squeal of joy. 'You naughty little ratties!' she whispered. 'Don't you dare run off like that again!'

Sheba looked at Sister Moon and rolled her eyes. There wasn't time for reunions. She led them out of the room and into the main corridor, which stretched all the way down the east wing.

The inside of the Great Exhibition was just as impressive as the exterior. Columns of iron stretched up, impossibly high, to the panels of the glass ceiling. Potted plants and small trees surrounded them, and there were thick carpets and drapes and banners everywhere. Exhibits lined the walkway on both sides. Sheba could see statues of tigers, horses and dragons, and people in costumes from all ages. Some even had no costumes on at all.

'Phwoar, look at this!' said Monkeyboy. He had clambered up to sit on the shoulders of a naked man and woman, their bits covered only by fig leaves.

'That's Adam and Eve, you disgusting child,' said Gigantus. 'Get down. We haven't got time to mess around.'

'This way to the diamond!' Sheba said, spotting a sign in the dim light. 'Hurry up!'

They began a hectic dash along the corridor, zipping past exhibits in a blur. Almost at the centre, they were stopped by Monkeyboy shouting again.

'Look at this! Look at this!'

'If you've stopped us to gawk at bronze boobies again,' began Gigantus, but quickly saw he was pointing at an object in what looked like an enormous birdcage, topped with a crown. Inside it, on a velvet cushion, was a diamond the size of a fist. The plaque beneath it read 'The Koh-i-Noor, Mountain of Light'. In the darkness of the empty exhibition it barely gave a twinkle. It could have just been a very expensive lump of glass.

'It's the diamond!' Sheba whispered. 'But why hasn't it been taken?'

Sister Moon drew her swords and looked around the shadows of the central court. The fountains were still, the main doors locked and barred. 'We early?' she suggested. 'Mrs Crowley not here yet?'

'Are you sure she said it was tonight, Sheba?' Mama Rat asked.

'I'm certain,' said Sheba.

'Unless that what she want you to think,' said Sister Moon.

'You mean we've just broken into the most important building in England for nothing?' Monkeyboy said. He stared around, wide-eyed, waiting for some kind of trap to be sprung. But there was nothing except the dark, the stillness and the blank stares of statues.

There was a long, uncomfortable silence. Sheba could feel everyone's eyes burning into her.

'I was *sure* it was the diamond,' she said, feeling helpless. 'Although she did laugh when I said it. But what else could she be after?'

'Well, we'd better do something soon, or a guard's going to come past and catch us standing here, and then we'll be on our way to the nearest prison,' Monkeyboy whispered.

Sheba nodded, miserably. She had been expecting to charge in and find Mrs Crowley, complete with all the mudlarks, in the act of stealing the diamond. *As if it was ever going to be that easy.*

'She must be here somewhere,' said Sister Moon, trying to be positive.

'I suggest we split up,' said Mama Rat, 'or we're never going to find her. And it's only a matter of time before someone spots the hole we cut. Then we've had it.'

Sister Moon scrambled up one of the columns to the first floor, and Monkeyboy copied her on the opposite side. Sheba marvelled at how they climbed: Monkeyboy as naturally as a real monkey, Sister Moon silent and graceful. She couldn't even see the tiny hand and footholds they used. They would search the galleries, then work their way down to the ground floor. Gigantus ran towards the west wing and Mama Rat headed south, towards the main entrance. Sheba watched them go. That left the north transept for her.

She began to step forward, then stopped suddenly.

She had felt something, a tingle in her nostrils.

There were many new and strange aromas inside the palace: machine oil, minerals, freshly varnished wood and foreign spices. But underneath them all was a hint of something else. Something sharp and cold.

Mrs Crowley. She was here.

Taking a deep breath, Sheba followed her nose.

The scent seemed to be coming from higher up, drifting down from the galleries on the first floor. Sheba tiptoed past the fountain and up the stairs. They led to a huge set of open doors. The ornate banner above it said 'India'.

There was a hint of moonlight from the glass ceiling overhead. Strange silhouettes loomed everywhere as Sheba stood in the doorway of the room, brought up short by a colossal, tusked monster, rearing up almost to the ceiling. Her hands shot to her mouth, holding back a scream, before she realised it was an elephant. A stuffed one, draped with embroidered silk and bearing a howdah big enough to house a small family. She stood still, trying to control her breathing, before padding cautiously into the room.

All around her were fabulous objects, decorated in the intricate and ornate Indian style. In the dim light she made out thrones and a beautiful tent crammed with carpets and cushions. There were spices, rocks and plants; a sample of everything the Indian soil could produce. The result was a sensory overload, an overpowering assault on Sheba's nose that made her head spin. And beneath that was the same nagging feeling of familiarity she'd had when she met Mrs Crowley, saw the clipper on the Thames, heard Baba Anish's accent. She had definitely smelt one of the odours before. Nose twitching, she followed the trail to a little plant in an earthen pot. It had a powerful, unmistakable scent, coming from its small white flowers. Flowers like the carved ones on her ebony box. Could that be why they were so familiar? They were labelled as jasmine, a native Indian plant. She must have come across them sometime in her unknown past. But how? She was a furry little orphan from a tatty seaside town in the middle of nowhere. What did she know of Indian flowers?

As if in answer she found herself remembering running through a white marble house . . . the air is hot around her, wide windows with billowing curtains fly past. She doesn't recognise the place — it's so grand! — but somehow she knows it. Her bare feet slap, slap, slap against the cool floor as she turns corner after corner. Now there's a courtyard. Ornamental ponds, water trickling between them. She can smell the jasmine. A distant voice calling her name . . . 'Sheba? Sheba? Is that you?' A figure sits beneath the shade of a palm. Wide skirts and a parasol. Another, more beloved scent. 'Mama . . .'

No! Pressing her hand over her mouth, Sheba dashed out of the Indian room.

She paused at the bottom of a flight of stairs, taking a

moment to calm herself. Away from the smell of spices and jasmine, her head began to clear. She was just anxious, she told herself. The tension was making her mind play tricks. If she could find Mrs Crowley, then all this would stop. As her senses returned to normal, she smelled once more the sharp, cold scent.

Sheba began to follow it again. She ran past a gallery full of farming implements, another dedicated to different forms of cutlery, and what looked like a room full of surgical implements. Now the scent was stronger still, and accompanied by a grinding noise from up ahead. It was a metallic sound, as if something was being cut. Her first thought was the bars of the Koh-i-Noor's birdcage, but that was far behind her now, back in the central court.

She took the clockwork pistol out from her cape. Sister Moon had tried to unjam it during their ride in the cab. But she hadn't had a chance to test it.

The room from which the noise came was titled 'Philosophical Instruments'. The scent was now unmistakably that of Mrs Crowley. She was in the room, and Sheba could smell neither the mudlarks nor the doctor. There was a dim glow inside. A lantern? The metallic grinding was quite loud now.

Sheba paused outside the doorway, as if an invisible barrier blocked her path. Should she go and get the others? But what if Mrs Crowley had gone by the time she got back? What if she had what she needed already and was about to leave?

There was no time for anything but action. She gathered

all her courage and stepped through the door, pistol raised.

The room was lined with display cases, all of them holding constructions of tubes, pipes, cogs, wire, dials and handles that looked immensely complicated. They could have been machines for making tea, shaving your eyebrows or summoning leprechauns for all Sheba knew. Standing in the centre of the room, holding a shuttered lantern, was a slender figure, dressed all in black.

Gone were the skirts, the bodice and the veil, but it was still unmistakeably Mrs Crowley. She now wore black trousers and a shirt with some kind of harness over the top. The bottom half of her face was covered by a black neckerchief, tied behind her head like a highwayman, and her eyes were hidden beneath the smoked glass lenses of a pair of goggles. Her black hair was pulled back in a tight bun and she was standing next to an exhibit which was clearly the centrepiece of the room. Unlike the others, it had been given its own cage, which Mrs Crowley was trying to break into. In her hands was some kind of automated saw, and the ground around her was littered with cut iron bars.

She looked up as Sheba entered. The white skin of her forehead wrinkled in a frown.

'You really are irritatingly persistent, aren't you?' she said.

'Stop what you're doing,' said Sheba. She couldn't quite keep her voice from shaking. 'Stop right now, or I'll shoot.'

'If you shoot me with your toy gun – presuming you

actually hit me, that is – then you'll never find the location of that pox-ridden girl you're looking for.' Sheba knew she was right. Even though she itched to pull the trigger, finding Till was more important.

'Besides,' Mrs Crowley continued. 'There is another very good reason why you shouldn't shoot me.'

'I can't think of one.' She lined the pistol sight up between the woman's eyes, just to keep her guessing whether she was going to do it.

'Have you ever wondered about your parents, Sheba? Has it ever puzzled you how you ended up a strange little freak, unwanted and all alone?'

Sheba's hands began to shake, the pistol jittering about. 'You don't know anything about me.' The woman was bluffing; lying again like she had about her stolen son.

'That's not entirely true,' Mrs Crowley continued. 'In fact, I know quite a bit. Would you like to hear it?'

'You're lying,' said Sheba. The tremble had spread to her voice. 'You've only met me twice before.'

'That was more than enough, my dear. How many girls like you can there be in the world? A little investigation proved my suspicions correct.'

'You don't know me!' Sheba shouted. 'Your servant tried to kill me!'

'He did, didn't he?' The woman raised a finger to her hidden lips as if it had been an innocent mistake. 'I must apologise. In hindsight, that was an error of judgement. I should have killed you myself.'

'You lied about your son, and you're lying now. You're nothing but an evil, murdering witch!' Sheba felt her teeth gnash and her eyes blaze as the fur stood out all over her face.

'I'm surprised you don't remember me, actually. Not my face, of course, but my voice at least. Do you remember the jasmine garden? The ornamental ponds? Or perhaps those long, white corridors you used to run up and down.'

Suddenly the room seemed very small and airless. Sheba's chest squeezed tight, making it hard for her to breathe. Her heart seemed to pound in her ears, and the only thing she could do was open her mouth and croak, 'No . . .'

'So you *do* remember. And how about your dear nanny? The poor young woman dragged from her home country, halfway across the world, to some cursed Indian hell-hole?'

'You?' Sheba managed to say. She had no memory of this woman, couldn't even imagine her as part of her past. But she knew about the white house. And that sweet undertone of Mrs Crowley's scent that was so familiar . . . Could there be any other explanation?

'Yes, me. Hard to believe, isn't it? But the things your family made me endure changed me in so many ways. To think I once ran around at the bidding of your stupid mother . . .'

'Mama . . .' Sheba's lip began to tremble. All those years of dreaming about her mother, and this woman might actually know where she was.

'Where is she?' Mrs Crowley read her mind. 'Who knows now? When you began to change . . . the shock nearly killed her. She was bed-ridden for months, and then one night she snatched you and left. The last I heard, she had boarded a clipper for England. Perhaps she blamed the foreign soil for her misfortunes. Maybe she wanted to escape your father. God knows she had reason enough. Who knows? She must have died on the journey home, leaving you an orphan. And now an exhibit in a tawdry sideshow, of all the things. How shameful.'

India, the ship, the memories. It all seemed to fit. What she had felt in the India room was no trick of the mind. It was a memory. A proper memory.

'Father?' Sheba managed to say, even as her legs buckled and she fell to the floor.

'I shouldn't spare a thought for him,' said Mrs Crowley. 'The brute wanted you locked away from the moment you started sprouting hair. After you and your mother left he became drunk, deranged. In the end I ended up caring for him like some pathetic nurse. Until I decided to pass myself off as his sister and take his fortune. After that he was useless. I'm glad I had Baba Anish slit his throat.'

'They're dead.' Sheba felt hot tears run down her cheeks. 'They're both dead.'

'Don't cry about it,' said Mrs Crowley, sounding disgusted. 'You never even knew them. Not really. You were a disgrace to them.'

Sheba didn't want to believe that was true. Why would her mother run away with her if she couldn't stand her? But part of what Mrs Crowley said was right. Crying over the loss of something you never had was stupid. Instead, she should be dealing with what she *did* have. This heartless criminal who had kidnapped the only normal friend Sheba had ever known. Thinking of Till stopped her tears. She still didn't know where the mudlarks were, or what the woman intended to do with them, but somehow she had to find out.

She watched as Mrs Crowley reached inside the display case and lifted out a box-like contraption. It had wire-coiled iron loops jutting from the top, with a series of metal discs in between. There were rods and cables poking out all over, and brass buttons and dials set into the mahogany casing.

That thing? Sheba thought. *That's what she's been after?*

Mrs Crowley tucked the device into a black canvas bag.

'Curious, are we? Wondering why it wasn't the diamond?'

'No,' Sheba said, a little too quickly. 'I just need to know what's been stolen when I scream for the police.'

'If you must know, it is Mr Faraday's Electromagnetic Impulse Generator. Not that I expect you to understand its importance.' Mrs Crowley heaved the bag onto her back and began clipping it to her harness. She watched Sheba closely the whole time. 'Given up on shooting me then, have you?'

'Why bother when the police can catch and question

you themselves? They'll find out where you've hidden the children.'

'I doubt that very much.' Mrs Crowley took a step backwards. Sheba could see a circular hole cut in the glass, much like the one Sister Moon had made, except this one had an indiarubber suction cup attached to it.

She climbed the wall, Sheba realised. *Like a giant, poisonous spider.*

'Why? You won't escape, you know. There are hundreds of soldiers and policemen out there.'

'Yes, but they're all going to be busy.' Mrs Crowley took a pocket watch from her belt and flipped it open. 'Right about *now*.'

From somewhere deep inside the exhibition came a thunderous bang, followed by the sound of hundreds of panes of glass exploding. The floor beneath them shook violently, setting all the exhibits rattling in their cases.

As Sheba threw herself to the floor, her first thought was for her friends, that one of them might have been caught by the blast. They might be lying there right now, as razor-sharp shards cascaded down. She had a sudden urge to dash back out of the room to find them all, to make sure they were safe.

But Mrs Crowley was moving again. She picked up a coil of black rope and tied it to the remains of the iron cage she had just dismantled. The other end she threw out of the hole.

'What about the children?' Sheba cried.

Mrs Crowley laughed, and squeezed through the hole

in the glass. There she paused, her feet braced on the side of the Crystal Palace.

'If you could see what I'm going to do with the children – what I could do for *you* – you wouldn't care less what happens to them, believe me. Follow me and see. If you dare.'

Then she slipped out of sight.

Sheba ran to the window and looked down to see her shadowy shape zipping down to the ground. Somewhere to her right was the red glow of fire, and hordes of men in army uniform were sprinting towards the Crystal Palace.

There was no time to find her friends and get them to safety. There was no way to stop the woman here and now without losing the children for ever. She had to make a decision.

Sheba grabbed the rope with one hand, put her foot on the edge of the glass hole, and jumped.

Chapter Eighteen

IN WHICH SHEBA GOES TO HOSPITAL.

Sheba spilled from the bottom of the rope and onto the grass with a thump that shook her entire body. All around was chaos, as smoke poured out from a shattered hole at the far west end of the exhibition. Men were swarming around it like angry bees round a kicked nest. She could hear the shouts and cries echoing.

She picked herself up and looked around in time to see a dark figure dashing away from the Crystal Palace toward the cover of the trees. Sprinting to keep up, Sheba scampered after her.

They ran through the shadows of Hyde Park, back

along Rotten Row. Crowds were starting to gather, come to stare at the burning Crystal Palace. Mrs Crowley wove through them, keeping close to the trees and bushes. She was wearing a cloak over her harness. Sheba struggled to follow, turning her head every now and then, hoping to see the other Peculiars amongst the throngs of gawkers.

But they were nowhere to be seen.

Near the park gates, Mrs Crowley finally slowed her pace. Sheba had a chance to catch up, although she had to keep straining on tiptoe to spot the woman amongst the crowds. *Can what she said be true?* she kept asking herself. *Was I really born in India?* It was too big to think about right now. First she had to find the mudlarks, discover what Crowley was up to, and *then* try and come to terms with it all. It would keep.

Finally, Mrs Crowley left the crowds and stepped out onto Hyde Park corner. A horse-drawn fire engine was negotiating its way through the gates, bells clanging. She calmly moved aside, the firemen not realising the very cause of the blaze was standing right next to them. Mrs Crowley crossed the road quickly towards a grand white building, its front covered with towering columns like all the other buildings nearby. She slipped around the side.

Sheba was still panting for breath after her sprint, but gritted her teeth and pushed against the gathering crowds to cross the street.

Outside the stately white mansion was a sign. It read 'St George's Hospital'. Hospitals, doctors. Sheba remembered Mrs Crowley's other servant. Could he be inside somewhere? Maybe the mudlarks, too?

She followed Mrs Crowley around the side of the mansion, and emerged behind it into a maze of much older, smaller buildings. Some were in the process of being demolished, scaffolding covering their sides in rickety cocoons, and the ground in between was covered with piles of bricks and worm-eaten timber.

Sheba spotted Mrs Crowley ducking under a tarpaulin and into one of these derelict buildings. Pulling her cape tight about her, Sheba followed.

It was dark inside, and filled with strange smells. Decades of dust, damp brick and plaster mingled with a mixture of medical odours. Sheba smelt dried blood, soap and starch; chemicals, medicines, disease and chamber pots. All of it was old and faded. A disused hospital, perhaps? A part of St George's once upon a time? There was a steep, winding staircase in front of her.

Mrs Crowley's footsteps echoed from somewhere above. Looking up, Sheba saw the woman's shadow moving round and round and up, the bulging pack jutting out like a hunched back.

She followed up the creaking steps – one, two, three floors – and then walked towards a door that glowed with flickering gaslight. Painted on the wall outside were the words 'Operating Theatre'. *Funny place to put on a show,* she thought, but when she peeked around the door she realised it was for a different kind of show entirely.

Mrs Crowley was in the centre of the room. She was unpacking Faraday's Electromagnetic Impulse Generator onto a workbench and, standing beside her, as excited as an infant on Christmas morning, was the doctor. Around them were more tables, these covered in saws and knives, vials, bottles, tubes and piping. But the whole scene was taking place in a lowered pit, surrounded by six or seven tiers of benches, all descending towards the stage space at the bottom.

It *was* a place for watching, Sheba realised. But the performance wasn't a Penny Gaff show. It was chopping and slicing and hacking. Surgery.

Sheba began to shake as she realised why Mrs Crowley might need a doctor and the mudlarks in a place like this. Something more vile and horrific than she could ever have imagined. And that was when she saw them. Bound and gagged and stacked in a pile at the back of the theatre. All ten children. Looming over them was another figure. It took Sheba a while to recognise him, as his face and hands were swathed in blood-spotted bandages, but when he looked up at her with those black-rimmed eyes she knew it couldn't be anyone else. *Baba Anish!* So much for him collapsing and getting thrown in the river.

'Come down, girl,' called Mrs Crowley, as if she had always known she was there. 'We are about to begin. And you will find this especially interesting.'

Sheba began to descend the stairs in the middle of the benches. Baba Anish watched her all the way. His jaw was oddly lopsided, held in place by a thick bandage surrounding his head, from which his matted locks spilled across his shoulders. Ignoring him, Sheba's eyes flicked all around, looking for something, anything that might help her put a stop to this.

'It's splendid, simply beautiful,' the doctor was fawning over the generator, rubbing his gangly hands over the mahogany casing.

Baba Anish was still gazing fiercely at her. He tried to shout something, but with his broken jaw so bandaged, all that came out was, 'Mmng ug ee ooing ere?'

'Hush,' said Mrs Crowley. 'Once I show her what we are about to do, we will have no more silliness, I'm sure. She's a resourceful girl. And she's here, after all. Maybe she'll make a good protégé. How long until we are ready, Doctor?'

The doctor adjusted a few switches on the generator, then turned the crank handle. The metal discs on the top began to whizz around, and blue crackles of light started jumping between the coils. This made the doctor clap his hands with glee, while Mrs Crowley and Baba Anish visibly flinched. Sheba stared, amazed. It was like watching tamed lightning. He took some copper wires from the rest of his apparatus on the bench and attached them to the generator. Then he turned to Mrs Crowley and gave a fawning bow. 'We are ready now, ma'am. We just need the first batch of ingredients.'

As if that were some prearranged signal, Baba Anish bent and hoisted up one of the mudlarks. He heaved the wriggling, squealing child towards the operating table.

Sheba recognised the big, brown eyes that stared at her above the gagged mouth. It was Till.

'Wait!' Sheba shouted. 'You haven't told me what you're doing yet! What's all this . . . all this stuff for?'

She pointed at the doctor's table, where the sparking generator was whirring away. Its cables led to a glass crucible on a stand, which was now starting to bubble, letting off a strong chemical stink.

'This, Sheba, is the miracle I was telling you about,' said Mrs Crowley. She took a clay pot from the table and removed the lid to reveal a grey, pulpy cream.

'It doesn't look much like a miracle to me,' said Sheba. The stuff stank – and it was the cold, sharp smell she had picked up from Mrs Crowley at the graveyard when they had first met.

'Haven't you ever despaired at your . . . condition?' Mrs Crowley asked. 'Haven't you ever wished away your cursed differences and dreamed of being normal? I know I have.'

As Sheba watched, Mrs Crowley reached up and removed her goggles. Underneath were surprisingly young eyes, elegantly shaped. Her nose was small, slightly upturned, but perfectly proportioned. She's beautiful, Sheba thought.

But then Mrs Crowley removed the black neckerchief.

From beneath her nose and down, the features were withered and shrunken. Her lips were gone, exposing jagged teeth hanging by threads in leathery gums. It was the face of someone long dead; a mummified corpse's mouth, like something you would find grinning up at you from an ancient grave.

'Pleasant, isn't it?' The distorted mouth gnashed as Mrs Crowley lisped the words. 'A souvenir of my time in India. Apparently it's a very rare affliction. According to Baba Anish, it means I've been blessed by his goddess. I should be honoured, shouldn't I?'

As Sheba stared in terror, trying not to scream, the woman dipped her fingers into the pot and smeared some of the grey goo onto her cheek. Instantly the withered skin started to change. It became plump, smooth and pale, like the rest of her face. Sheba let out a little gasp of amazement. She couldn't believe what she was seeing. It was like some kind of magic.

'Try some,' said Mrs Crowley. 'With this, both of us could be normal. Neither of us need hide ourselves away again. Not ever.' She took hold of Sheba's hand and smeared a dab onto the back. As Sheba stared, she felt her flesh beginning to tingle. When she rubbed her thumb over it, the hair fell away, revealing soft, pink skin underneath.

It works! Sheba thought. For a few perfect seconds, her mind spun with all the wonderful possibilities. No more freak shows. No more hiding from the world in the shadows of her hood. Being able to walk down the street and talk to people, really talk to them, without them running away screaming.

'But the effects are only temporary,' said Mrs Crowley.

Already, her patch of cheek was beginning to wrinkle

and shrink, and when Sheba looked down she could see minute hairs pushing their way out of her skin again. Mrs Crowley tied the neckerchief back around her mouth.

'That is why we are here today,' she said. 'The doctor has found a means to make the change permanent.'

'Yes,' said the doctor, blinking his eyes behind the huge lenses of his spectacles. 'The problem is in the subject material. I discovered that only children's would work, but dead ones were all I could obtain from the Resurrection Men – bodysnatchers or grave-robbers, you might call them. I realised that, to make the cream have permanent effect, I would need live tissue to combine with my compound. That, and a substantial electrical charge to "activate" the cells. To bring them to life, as it were. I tried a range of generating devices of my own design, but I couldn't create a powerful enough current. That is why we required Faraday's engine, here. A spectacular piece of engineering. Truly revolutionary. I think the man only realised its potential himself recently, which is why he was about to remove it from the exhibition.'

'What material are you talking about?' asked Sheba, trying to keep calm. 'What is it you're taking from the children?'

'Why, brains, of course!' The doctor looked at her as if she were stupid. 'Precisely, the cells from the brain stem. In the correct solution, and with an electrical impulse to stimulate them, they somehow repair the body's cells. Make them "normal" again.'

Sheba suddenly realised she had some cream on her

hand still. With a shudder, she wiped it off on her dress.

'But the children,' she said, trying to keep her voice from trembling. 'If you cut their brains out, they'll die!'

'And what of it?' said Mrs Crowley. 'They are only starving urchins. Life is wasted on them. It's likely none of them will live to adulthood, anyway, and if they do, what will their useless lives achieve? The breeding of even more diseased paupers?'

The doctor picked up a jagged silver saw that looked sharp enough to cut through bone.

'This is just a small sacrifice so that I can go on to achieve much greater things,' said Mrs Crowley. 'And you can join me, free from that hideous affliction which has landed you in a degrading freak show. You should be on your knees, thanking me for this opportunity.'

Sheba looked at the terrified face of Till, strapped to the table and about to have the top of her head sliced off like a boiled egg.

'No!' she cried. 'Never! You can't do this. It's wrong!'

Before she could reach for her pistol, or run at the insane doctor, she felt a pair of huge, steely hands close about her arms. It was Baba Anish. She hadn't even noticed him get behind her.

'Pity,' said Mrs Crowley. 'Too sentimental, that's your problem. Just like your pathetic mother.' She looked at Baba Anish, who Sheba could feel growling behind her. 'Make her watch this first one,' she said. 'Then you can send her to your goddess.'

Baba Anish held Sheba tight as the doctor moved closer

to Till and lowered the saw to her head. Mrs Crowley stood nearby, holding a metal basin and some kind of slicing scoop.

'We have to be quick,' the doctor was saying. 'The tissue must be placed in the charged solution before the cells start to decay.'

His words seemed to echo in Sheba's ears as if he were drifting far away. Suddenly she felt very hot, and it was difficult to breathe. The blood pounded and thrummed in her head, each heartbeat seemed to last a minute, and she realised she was fainting. *Stay awake!* she screamed to herself. *Stay awake and do something!*

She saw the teeth of the bone saw pressing against Till's forehead. She saw little drops of blood form as they dug into her tender skin. She saw the doctor's goggling eyes, focused on their horrid task. A tiny bead of sweat was creeping down his temple at the speed of a snail.

She saw Mrs Crowley's eyes crinkling at the corners, as if that hideous mouth of hers was smiling underneath its black silk neckerchief.

And then she saw something silver flash across the table. It thudded into the doctor's arm, sending tiny teardrops of blood flying outwards, like a red rose unfurling.

It was followed by a bang that made Sheba's ears ring, and Mrs Crowley fell backwards in slow motion, the bowl and scoop she was holding flying up into the air. Sheba's terrified mind couldn't fathom what was happening. All she could do was stare at the doctor's arm. The thing that had hit him was shaped like a star. A perfect silver star twinkling in the gaslight.

How on earth did a shooting star get in here? her addled mind wondered.

And then she understood, and with understanding time sprang back to normal.

She looked up.

Sister Moon perched on one of the wooden benches, drawing another throwing star from her belt.

Mama Rat stood on the steps, rats clustered about her shoulders, smoking flintlock pistol in her hand.

Behind them came Gigantus, yelling a battle cry, and Monkeyboy clinging to his back, face white with terror.

'You're here!' Sheba shouted, tears of joy in her eyes. 'You're safe!'

Behind her, Baba Anish let out a muffled roar. He moved one hand from her shoulder to draw his sword, and Sheba took her chance. She sank her needle-sharp fangs into his other wrist and then, when he let go with a roar of surprise, sprinted to the other side of the theatre.

'Save Till!' she shouted at her friends.

Even as the Peculiars ran down the steps to where Sheba stood, the doctor was already turning to flee. Wailing with terror, he paused to snatch the generator from the table, scattering and smashing bottles everywhere in the process, and ran out of a narrow side door. Mrs Crowley pulled herself up and followed him, slamming the little door behind her. Mama Rat's shot had hit her side and she clutched it as she ran.

'Get the others!' Sister Moon shouted. 'I take the painted man!'

The bandaged hulk drew his curved sword. He moved towards Sister Moon as she unsheathed both her swords and moved into a fighting stance. Sheba ran to the door, but found it locked tight. She frantically searched for a keyhole to pick, but Gigantus gently moved her aside.

'Quicker if I break it, I think.'

As the big man started to pound on the door, Sheba turned to watch Sister Moon fight the Indian.

Baba Anish had looked murderous before, but now he was horrific. The paint daubed around his eyes was criss-crossed with fresh red cuts from the window glass he had been thrown through. His nose was squashed and crooked, the nostrils caked with dried blood. He looked at Sister Moon with a fury hot enough to melt lead, then, with a lung-rending howl, he launched himself at her, his sword whistling through the air, forcing her further up the stairs to the plate-glass windows at the very back.

As he charged, Moon let him come, opening her guard purposefully. Just as he began his deathstrike, she placed a foot in the centre of his chest and let herself fall backwards onto the floor. His momentum carried him over her head, and at exactly the right moment she kicked hard with her leg and sent him soaring through the air. The old plate window was directly behind them, and for the second time that day, Baba Anish flew straight through the glass, smashing it with his face. With a disbelieving wail, he vanished into the foggy night, on his way to the ground at unpleasantly high speed.

Sister Moon rolled to her feet, calmly returning to the *seiza* stance.

'*That* for Matthew the rat,' she said.

Sheba cheered, just as Gigantus broke open the door with a final blow. Weapons drawn, the Peculiars ran full pelt after Mrs Crowley.

Sheba sprinted down the crumbling corridors after the fleeing forms of the doctor and Mrs Crowley. She saw them turn, heading through an open door to her right, and moments later she skidded through it herself.

She emerged into a wide room, floorboards covered with brick dust and rubble. The doctor and Crowley were standing in the far corner, both gripping Faraday's generator.

'We had an agreement, you fool!' Mrs Crowley was screaming. 'You can have the machine *after* you've cured me!'

'But those freaks!' the doctor yelled back. 'They will kill us! Look at my arm!'

'Stop right there!' Sheba shouted from the doorway. She had her pistol out again, and this time there was no hesitation. She fired a shot and the dart pinged across the room to hit the doctor right in the middle of his bald head. He instantly froze, clutching the generator in a rigor mortis grip.

'Paralysis dart,' Sheba said, as Gigantus and Mama Rat arrived behind her.

Mrs Crowley let out a throat-wrenching scream of fury. With shaking hands, she pulled out a box of lucifer matches and fumbled to strike one.

'What's she doing now?' asked Monkeyboy. 'Smoking a pipe?'

Sheba made a move across the room, just as Mrs Crowley managed to light a match. She gave Sheba a last, hate-filled glance, then threw the flaming stick onto the floor. There was a hissing sound, and a cloud of stinking, sulphurous smoke.

'Gunpowder!' Mama Rat shouted. 'The building is booby-trapped!'

Sheba watched in horror as a trail of fire zipped along the side of the room. She could now see a line of black powder that must have been set out earlier, just in case the evil woman needed to make an escape. It would probably lead to a keg somewhere; enough black powder to bring the crumbling old building down around them.

She should have been filled with terror. She should have turned and run from the building. Instead she was filled with a sudden rush of anger. This woman, who had destroyed her family, hurt her friends, was about to escape into the night. There was no way she could let that happen.

She felt the fur on her face stand and thicken. Her jaw stretched, her teeth sliding into spiked points. Time seemed to slow down. She casually noticed how her hands had squeezed themselves into paws, and she felt an irresistible urge to howl. *This is it*, she thought, *I've finally become a proper wolf.* She was surprised to find that this time she didn't care.

As the gunpowder ignited with a boom that shook the walls and threw the other Peculiars to the ground, Sheba fell on all fours and began to bound across the room towards Mrs Crowley.

There was fire and smoke everywhere. The explosion had come from the floor beneath, thrusting jagged floorboards up like splintered mountain ranges. It cracked the walls and sent bricks, slates and chunks of timber raining from the ceiling.

Sheba dodged all these with preternatural speed, jinking and swerving across the floor. Mrs Crowley was at a door in the room's corner, forcing it open whilst still trying to drag the generator from the doctor's grip. The smoke in front of her parted, and the snarling form of Sheba came flying through.

Mrs Crowley gave an uncharacteristic squeal as Sheba landed in front of her. Letting go of the generator, she aimed a kick at the little wolfgirl's head. Sheba dodged out of the way, and sank her teeth into the woman's ankle.

'You vicious animal!' Mrs Crowley screamed. She reached down and grabbed Sheba by the hair, hauling her head up. In her state of rage, all Sheba wanted to do was bite again. She was almost too frenzied to notice the glinting thing that had appeared in Mrs Crowley's hand. The woman had a knife and was swinging it down towards her throat.

Sheba tried to pull away, but her hair was held tight.

The knife drew closer, cutting through the smoke in slow motion, now centimetres away from her neck. With wide eyes, Sheba saw the triumphant grin forming on Mrs Crowley's face; one that rapidly changed to horror as something small and betailed bounced off the nearest wall and onto her head.

'Monkeyboy!' Sheba shouted.

Mrs Crowley screamed as the little imp perched on her shoulders, slapping and punching at her face. Sheba was about to help him, when the floor beneath her gave a violent lurch.

She looked down. The floorboards had given way, opening up a fire-filled hole to the floor below. For one horrible moment she teetered, about to spill down into the flames, and then a hand was on her shoulder. It was Sister Moon, face smeared with soot. And then the ninja was pulling her clear, back through the smoke to safety.

They dashed back across the room, dodging holes and falling bricks, until they were back at the far door again. Mama Rat and Gigantus were waiting for them and a few seconds later, Monkeyboy appeared, coughing and spluttering.

'She threw me off,' he managed to say. 'The slippery mare got away!'

Sheba didn't care. They all crowded round, wrapping their arms about each other, filled with an inexpressible joy that they were all safe and together again.

'The mudlarks!' Sheba shouted, breaking free of the huddle. 'We have to get them out!'

Everyone instantly turned to run back to the operating theatre, rushing to free the children before the fire took hold. Sheba followed, but not before sparing a backward glance through the smoke to where the hazy silhouette of the doctor stood, still paralysed, and behind him the empty doorway through which Mrs Crowley had escaped.

The Peculiars herded the gaggle of dazed mudlarks out of the burning building. Till turned to Sheba and gave her a tight, fierce hug. The other children were just as grateful. They thronged each other and the Peculiars in a tearful huddle, unable to believe their long ordeal was finally over.

Sheba felt like collapsing onto the ground and gulping in mouthfuls of the clear night air, but she knew they couldn't stand around for long. It was only a matter of time before the police, already out in their hundreds, came to investigate the explosion.

'We have to go,' she said, her voice croaky with smoke. The others nodded, and keeping to the shadows, the group headed out of the hospital grounds, passing the crumpled form of Baba Anish as they went.

Part of Sheba wanted to stay and tell the police what had happened. They might be in time to rescue the doctor and the generator. They might be able to catch Mrs Crowley and bring her to justice.

But it was more likely they would laugh in their faces, all the way to the nearest cells. They were nothing but a gaggle of rag-tag sideshow freaks after all. And, at the very worst, they might even think they had stolen the generator themselves. Judging by all the police and soldiers, the theft was being treated as a matter of national security, and Sheba didn't really fancy her head being stuck on a spike on top of Temple Bar.

No, it was better that nobody knew they were involved. They had stopped Mrs Crowley and saved the children. That was all that mattered. As the first policemen came running, blowing their whistles and shouting for help, Sheba and the others slipped through the crowds on Hyde Park corner and home, to Brick Lane, with Till clutching Sheba's hand all the way.

Chapter Nineteen

IN WHICH SHEBA FINDS HER HOME.

The morning edition of *The Times* was full of speculation about the events in Hyde Park. The front page showed a drawing of the Crystal Palace with flames rising from a gaping hole in its side, and beneath it the article read:

Burglary and Bombs at the Great Exhibition

At around midnight last night, Hyde Park was host to a tragic spectacle. The Crystal Palace, site of the Great Exhibition of the Works of Industry of All Nations, fell victim to a malicious and cowardly attack.

Persons unknown managed to gain access to the North Gallery by cutting through the *glass wall*. They then removed at least one of the exhibits, before placing an explosive device in the Refreshment Court. Thanks to the diligence and bravery of London's Fire Brigades, none of the displays was lost.

Prince Albert himself is due to inspect the damage this morning, and it is expected the exhibition will remain closed for at least two days.

There was also a piece on the theft, which Sheba read eagerly:

Failed attempt to steal Faraday's Generator

It seems that the target of last night's raid on the Great Exhibition was the Electromagnetic Impulse Generator, designed and built by Mr Michael Faraday, one of the Exhibition judges.

A revolutionary new design, the Generator is capable of creating the strongest electrical impulses yet achieved, with its inventor claiming that one day similar machines will replace steam and water power throughout the nation.

Ultimately, however, the plot was foiled: The criminals chose one of the derelict buildings of the old St George's Hospital as their lair, which then caught fire. The first policemen on the scene discovered the missing device, and also apprehended two criminals. One was a Doctor Everard Whitmore of Rotherhithe, the other an unknown foreigner who is thought to be a mystic.

Both men were severely injured and are now in police custody, while the generator has been returned to Mr Faraday.

Sheba folded the paper and placed it back on the kitchen table. She was glad it had all turned out all right, but couldn't help a twinge of envy. *It should have been us in the papers,* she thought. Instead nobody would ever know who had *really* stopped Mrs Crowley.

Although that wasn't quite true. The parlour at Brick Lane was full of little sleeping people who would remember. They filled up most of the floor space, curled around each other, gently snoring. And after all, everything the Peculiars had done hadn't really been anything to do with foiling burglaries or catching criminals. It had been about keeping those children safe.

Sheba hopped down from the table and started to stoke up the stove, ready to put some coffee on for breakfast.

A few hours later, everyone was sitting in the front room, talking about the events of the night before. Upstairs in the bedroom, Gigantus had hauled up the tin bath and filled it with water from the street pump, warmed over the fire. The mudlarks were taking it in turns to have the first bath of their lives, and the sounds of whoops and splashes drifted down every now and then.

'But what happened when the bomb went off?' Sheba was asking. 'How come none of you were hurt?'

'Luck, I suppose,' said Mama Rat. 'It just happened none of us was near it at the time. If we hadn't split up to find that woman, it might have been a different story.'

'And how did you get out without being caught? The place was crawling with soldiers when I left.'

'We all ran back to the east wing when we heard the blast,' said Gigantus. He was writing in his notebook again, pen scratching across the paper, just as if the events of the past few days had never happened. 'The guards were so busy with the fire, we managed to slip out of Sister Moon's hole in the glass and join the crowds.'

'And then we find this,' said Sister Moon. She held up the chipped marble that Till had given her. 'It must fall from your pocket. Before that, we think you stuck in Exhibition, or hurt by bomb. Then Monkeyboy spot you running down Rotten Row.'

'That was very clever of you, Monkey,' said Sheba, as he puffed out his chest.

'I know,' he said, beaming.

'We watched you following Mrs Crowley into that old hospital,' said Mama Rat. 'We would have caught up to you sooner, had it not been so crowded. Thank goodness we got there in time. What you did was very brave, though, Sheba.'

Sheba blushed beneath her fur. She didn't know what to say. She was saved from further embarrassment by the mudlarks coming down the stairs. It was strange to see them so clean and happy; they were like a completely different group of children. Sheba could see their faces properly now, without the coating of mud. There were rosy cheeks, freckles and happy smiles. They looked more like a school class on an outing than a bunch of kidnap victims, recently saved from certain death.

'I'll get some soup on,' said Mama Rat. 'Feed you lot up a bit. Won't be long until Large 'Arry reads my little message, if Bartholomew rat gets his skates on.'

Not long after that there was a knock at the door. Sister Moon opened it to reveal a group of nervous-looking figures, clad in shapeless, muddy rags. They were bowing and scraping, and trying to peep past Sister Moon at the same time.

Sheba recognised Till's ma and pa, along with another boy who might have been Barney Bilge (it was difficult to tell, because last time she saw him, he had been completely covered in wet mud). Behind them were even more people, all clutching their caps in their hands and chattering excitedly.

When Moon stepped aside, they all rushed though and gathered the children in such tight embraces that Sheba began to worry their stick-thin limbs might snap. The parlour was full to bursting, and the Peculiars found themselves pushed back against the stairs. But it was a heart-warming sight, and Sheba felt a lump in her throat, especially now she knew such a reunion would never be hers.

Her father was dead, her mother lost and her family fortune stolen by Mrs Crowley. She had nothing left. Not even the hope-filled daydreams of a normal life. It was like everything she had ever wanted had just been dangled before her eyes, only to be snatched away again. For ever.

She glanced up to see Gigantus blinking rapidly and pretending to look at something on the ceiling. She silently offered him her hanky, then had to wring the sodden little piece of cloth out after he gave it back.

'Your amazing worshipfulnesses . . .' said Till's father, as soon as the hugging and kissing was over. 'I 'as got no idea 'ow we is ever going to fank you. We never fought we'd see our dear little 'uns again, and now 'ere they are, all bathed and everything! I never imagined a child of mine would live to 'ave a proper barf.'

'You're welcome,' said Sheba, Monkeyboy and Sister Moon together. Seeing the reunion made everything they'd been through seem worthwhile.

'I knew you'd come through for us,' said the father mudlark. 'We is so used to losing young 'uns to the river and the sickness and a hundred other things. It's our way of life, and no one but us seems to care. We didn't expect you to, neither, but I'm very glad to say we was wrong.'

Sister Moon bowed gracefully, while the rest of them just beamed. Most of the other families left with their children, after shaking the Peculiars' hands in turn. Till's family hung back after the rest, and accepted Mama Rat's offer of tea. They stayed for most of the afternoon, listening with rapt fascination as the Peculiars recounted the story of the rescue. As Sheba heard it retold, she was struck by how incredible it sounded, but the mudlarks never once questioned it. They only stopped every now and then to wail in terror or sympathy, or to heap excessive praises on each of the Peculiars in turn. They even had the decency not to stare too much, although she did notice Till's ma absent-mindedly stroking her cheeks when she looked at her, as if she was wondering what a coat of fur would feel like.

At the end of the story, they all broke into applause and

Till hugged Sheba tightly again.

'What will you do now?' Sheba asked. She didn't like the thought of her new friend going back to a life of dangerous scavenging, even if there were no longer strange mechanical creatures lurking in the mud.

'Well, miss,' said the father mudlark, 'first, we is going to thank Large 'Arry for all his help. Then meself, the missus, Till and 'er brothers will be leaving the city.'

'Leaving?' Till and Sheba said together.

'Yes,' said Till's mother. 'I 'ave a cousin what works on a farm down in Kent. A place called Stanhope Farm. She's always said there's room for us there. The children can work picking hops, and Tam and me can labour on the farm.'

'It'll be a better life for us all,' said the father.

Till looked at Sheba with tearful eyes. 'I won't ever see you again, will I?'

Sheba shook her head, too heartbroken to speak.

'I don't know about that,' said Mama Rat.

'Aye. We often go down that way in the summer, when the fayres are on,' added Gigantus.

'We find a way to make Plumpscuttle go to Kent,' said Sister Moon.

'Just as long as there's something to eat besides turnips,' Monkeyboy added. 'My arse can't handle all that again.'

'Promise you'll come see me,' Till said, squeezing Sheba's hands. 'Promise!'

'I will, I promise!' Sheba said, laughing. Next summer

was a long way away, but it was better than nothing.

With that, the mudlarks prepared to leave. Before heading out of the door, they bowed and smiled at each of the Peculiars in turn, so that Sheba began to feel as though she was some kind of royalty. As she watched them disappear down Brick Lane on the way back to the river, she held the chipped marble Till had given her when they had first met. She looked at it for a moment, squeezed it tight, then took it upstairs to place inside her ebony box.

Afterwards, she sat for a long time, running her fingers over the carved jasmine flowers. *This box must have come from India, too*, she thought. *Perhaps it was my mother's?* It made her think again of Mrs Crowley's story, opening everything up like a fresh wound. Those little, star-shaped flowers, just like the ones at the Exhibition. But she had seen them somewhere else recently, too. Where had it been?

Shortly after that, they received another visitor, a messenger this time from the London Hospital. He brought them a note that said Plumpscuttle had almost fully recovered, and would be returning the next day.

The Peculiars all groaned. Without the gluttonous Plumpscuttle, their little house was quite a pleasant place to live. Now they would have to return to being slaves and exhibits.

'We should have charged those mud-sloppers a blooming fortune. Then we could have done a runner while fat ginger-knickers was on his sickbed,' said Monkeyboy, as he stomped off to his cage to sulk.

'And what would they have paid us with, exactly?' said

Gigantus. 'Half a ton of raw sewage?'

'I'd rather have a load of rotten poo than that blubbery bully, any day,' Monkeyboy called back from the yard.

Sheba was inclined to agree. Still, a free afternoon gave her time to run a little errand or two.

Leaving the others to repair the house as much as possible, she padded upstairs to fetch something hidden under a certain strongman's bed. While he was still scribbling in his journal, she slipped out of the house.

After making a brief stop-off in Whitechapel, Sheba caught an omnibus south of the river. She sat in the furthest corner, squashed against the side by a plump businessman in a stovepipe hat. Her hood was pulled low over her face, and she clutched the pennies she had borrowed from Mama Rat in her fist, waiting for the conductor. She was terrified she might miss her stop and end up lost in London, but there wasn't time to walk to her destination and back.

When the omnibus finally pulled up at a riverside tavern called The Angel, Sheba was glad to escape its cramped, sweaty confines and stretch her legs. She took a moment to look out at the river, safe now – at least from Baba Anish and his machine – thanks to her and her friends. Although none of the hundreds of people working, steaming and sailing up and down the Thames right now knew a thing about it.

She could have stood there all day, working up the courage for what she had to do. Instead she forced her feet to walk along the Rotherhithe Wall and turn down Love Lane. A little further on, and she emerged on Paradise Street. A few doors down on her left was number 17.

Just as before, she slipped around the back and opened the lock with her hairpins. Just as before, her breath came quick and shallow, as she imagined Mrs Crowley sitting inside, waiting for her. *But she wouldn't be stupid enough to come back*, Sheba told herself. *Would she?*

The house was silent and still again, although this time shards of daylight slipped in through the grimy windows, filling the air with glowing motes of dust. Sheba tiptoed through the kitchen and up the stairs, all the while clutching the pistol in her coat pocket, just in case.

When she reached the third floor, she paused. There was the keyhole she had spied through. There was the room they had hidden in and there, on the dirty floorboards, was a rusty puddle of dried blood where Matthew had met his end.

Sheba had been thinking a lot about this place. She had been thinking especially of the paintings in that room, of the carved wood that framed them.

She took a deep breath and walked to the door, pushing it wide, then stepped in to the room, pistol raised.

The high-backed armchair was there, a dark shape in the middle. Sheba squeezed the trigger, shooting a dart. There was a soft *pop* of bursting leather as it hit the empty chair back. There was nothing there: just shadow.

Breathing a sigh of relief, Sheba looked around the room. Someone *had* been here, and they had left in a hurry. The furniture was toppled and strewn; everything of value had been taken. Mrs Crowley had gone.

But the paintings were still there.

Sheba moved closer, looking at the frames first. They were made of dark ebony and all around them were twining jasmine flowers. Just like the ones on her box.

Now that she knew, she took her time stepping backwards and looking up. She was finally going to meet her parents.

Her father was a stern, proud-looking man. He wore the red uniform of the British army, his chest covered with medals. The dusty hills behind him must be somewhere in India. Maybe the place Sheba grew up. She tried to imagine him drunk and raving, as Mrs Crowley had described. But he didn't look weak enough. And to let that woman take everything from him . . .

It was too painful to think about. Instead, she turned to her mother. She was beautiful, so beautiful it made Sheba cry. She wore a dress of white silk and gazed out of the picture with a kind, loving smile. And her eyes. They were the same shape, the same amber colour as hers. She recognised her now. Remembered her.

Sheba gazed at the painting, wanting to take in every detail before she left. She memorised her mother's hair, the shape of her nose, her lips. And her hands . . . She peered closer, her heart beating just a little faster. Were the nails slightly pointed? Almost claw-like?

Sheba clutched her own hands together, squeezing hard. Could her mother have been like her? Would she really have been ashamed of her daughter, like Mrs Crowley said? Deep in her bones, Sheba knew it wasn't true. After all, she'd taken Sheba with her when she had left India. She would never really know why she had come to England, but that wasn't important. All that mattered was that she had taken Sheba with her.

It was time to go now. There would be many hours to think over her parents and what might have happened to them. Sheba wished she could pack up the portraits and take them with her, but they were too huge, and would involve too much explaining. For now, this was her secret. She would leave them here in this dusty house, knowing she could come back to see them whenever she wished. That was good enough.

Later on, at suppertime, the Peculiars gathered around the kitchen table for their last free meal without Plumpscuttle. Out in the yard, Raggety and Flossy had an extra helping of oats, and Sheba ladled out Penny Dip into bowls as Sister Moon handed them around.

Mama Rat was beaming. The other rats had brought her a present that morning: a greasy little baby rat they had found abandoned in a sewer somewhere. She was feeding it little scraps of chewed meat.

'I'm going to call you Paul,' she cooed, as the scraggly thing let out a piteous mewl.

Sheba concentrated on keeping down her mutton.

Monkeyboy was in an uncommonly good mood, too. He was telling everyone about his heroics of the other night in great detail. Something had also pleased Sister Moon. Whether it was rescuing the children, or getting the better of Baba Anish, Sheba couldn't tell, but her smile was especially serene.

The only person who wasn't in a jubilant mood was Gigantus. He was obviously having trouble with his writing, and kept scribbling out passages in his journal in between mouthfuls. Sheba thought she knew what would cheer him up, though.

When the stew was finished, she stood on her stool and cleared her throat.

'If you please,' she said, 'I have an announcement to make.'

All eyes turned to her.

'Today I took the book Gigantus has been writing—'

'You did *what?!*' The big man jumped from his stool, his face going pink with rage.

But Sheba carried on. 'I took your book and showed it to the printers on Whitechapel Road,' she said. 'I'm really sorry, but when I found it – by accident, of course – I just couldn't stop reading it. It deserves better than being hidden under your mattress, Gigantus. And the printers thought so too. They read it there and then, and they want to publish it in their magazine.'

'My book?' said Gigantus. 'It's going to be published? In a real magazine?'

He stood silent, face impassive and steely eyes fixed on Sheba in a frown. She began to wonder if she might have done something really stupid when Gigantus suddenly rushed around the table at her. She screwed her eyes shut and flinched, but instead of pounding her into paste, he grabbed her in a huge bear hug.

'Thank you,' he said, tears in his eyes. 'I should be furious with you, but thank you. *Thank you.*'

'Are you going to publish it in your own name?' Sheba asked, when the big man had finally let go.

'I don't think Gabriel Greepthick would go down too well,' he said. 'Gertrude Lacygusset is much better.'

'Gabriel!' Monkeyboy screamed with laughter. 'That's a girl's name!'

'Well, it's better than Timbert Tibbs,' said Gigantus. He looked as if he regretted opening his mouth.

'I don't actually know any of your *real* names,' said Sheba. It was something she'd never even thought about.

'Akiko,' said Sister Moon, bowing.

'And I'm Marie,' said Mama Rat. 'And how about you, dearie? Do you know *your* real name?'

'It's Sheba,' she said. 'I know that now for sure. Sheba is the name my mother gave me.'

'Well, now we've all been properly introduced, I think it's high time for a celebration,' said Mama Rat.

The rest of the Peculiars cheered.

At least until they heard the front door slam.

Plumpscuttle's gurgling baritone yelled at them from the parlour.

'What, in the name of Prince Albert's moustache, has happened to my pigging front door? And why does my house stink like a week-old chamber pot? Has someone been carving chunks out of my wall? And the bath is out! Who said you lot could have a bath? Get out here and explain yourselves!'

Plumpscuttle's stay in hospital had done nothing to improve his temper. His face was still puffy and bruised, and thick bandages could be seen beneath his shirt. The thing that seemed to have annoyed him most, however, was having had to eat cabbage soup instead of five dinners.

He spent the best part of an hour insulting the Peculiars, before stamping up the stairs to his bedroom. Then he noticed the blanket covering the smashed window, and came back down to shout all over again. Finally he left them to get ready for a show, 'to pay for all the chuffing damage to the house'.

For once they all joined Monkeyboy in making rude gestures behind his back. Then they set about putting up the sheets and tarpaulins for showtime.

By the time Plumpscuttle's dozy nephew turned up to man the door, they were just hanging up the last string of lanterns. Phineas stood watching them mutely, while he rooted around in his left nostril with a pudgy finger. Right on cue, Plumpscuttle emerged from his room dressed in an almost-clean suit. He was verging on cheerful, clearly glad at being out of the less-than-hygienic hospital ward.

The Peculiars shuffled off to their various parts of the house, ready for the show to begin.

Sheba sat on her little stool in the corner of their bedroom. She stared glumly at the sheets hanging in front of her, watching as the silhouette of Sister Moon moved in a graceful ballet with her twin sword blades tracing arcs and spirals, and listening to the sounds of the others going through their acts. A few hours ago she had been fighting villains and rescuing lost children, and now she was sitting like a sack of potatoes, waiting for people to shriek at the sight of her.

As the first customers came thumping up the stairs, she tried to drum up the enthusiasm to make herself look as freakish as possible. It wasn't working. Once you had spent a few days fighting hand to hand with twisted machines and evil forces, sitting in a sideshow seemed astoundingly dull. *I'm so much more than just a lonely freak now*, she thought. *I'm part of a team. And I have a mother that loves me. Or at least I did.*

The realisation made her pull herself upright and jut out her chin. Her fur bristled, and she let her growing canines pop out over her lip. Let these people gawp and whisper at her if they wanted. How many of them had saved children and stopped evil maniacs?

And even better, now she had something she had never dreamed possible. She had a family of her own. Maybe not the most conventional or normal, but a family nonetheless.

Sheba picked up her ivory comb and began to run it through her chestnut-brown curls, taking out the tangles. She looked out over the rooftops of London and smiled. Everyone always said she had a lovely head of hair.

ACKNOWLEDGEMENTS

Huge thanks to Claire and Marek for all their support, and also to everyone at Chicken House, especially my amazing editors Imogen Cooper, Rachel Leyshon and Christine O'Brien.

BEETLE BOY by M. G. LEONARD

Darkus can't believe his eyes when a huge insect drops out of the trouser leg of his horrible new neighbour. It's a giant beetle – and it seems to want to communicate.

But how can a boy be friends with a beetle? And what does a beetle have to do with the disappearance of his dad and the arrival of Lucretia Cutter, with her taste for creepy jewellery?

'A darkly funny Dahl-esque adventure.'
KATHERINE WOODFINE, AUTHOR

'A wonderful book, full to the brim with very cool beetles!'
THE GUARDIAN

Paperback, ISBN 978-1-910002-70-4, £6.99 • ebook, ISBN 978-1-910002-98-8, £6.99

WHO LET THE GODS OUT? by MAZ EVANS

When Elliot wished upon a star, he didn't expect a constellation to crash into his dungheap. Virgo thinks she's perfect. Elliot doesn't. Together they release Thanatos, evil Daemon of Death. Epic fail.

They need the King of the Gods and his noble steed. They get a chubby Zeus and his high horse Pegasus.

Are the Gods really ready to save the world? And is the world really ready for the Gods?

'. . . lashings of adventure, the Olympic gods as you've never seen them before and a wonderfully British sense of humour.'
FIONA NOBLE, THE BOOKSELLER

Paperback, ISBN 978-1-910655-41-2, £6.99 • ebook, ISBN 978-1-910655-64-1, £6.99

THE SECRET KEEPERS by TRENTON LEE STEWART

A magical watch. A string of secrets. A race against time.

When Reuben discovers an old pocket watch, he soon realizes it has a secret power: fifteen minutes of invisibility. At first he is thrilled with his new treasure, but as one secret leads to another, he finds himself on a dangerous adventure full of curious characters, treacherous traps and breathtaking escapes. Can Reuben outwit the sly villain called The Smoke and his devious defenders the Directions and save his city from a terrible fate?

'There are some genuinely haunting and ingenious moments as the three young heroes combat the villain in his mouldy mansion.'
THE NEW YORK TIMES

'. . . the tension never flags and the hold-your-breath moments come thick and fast.'
CAROUSEL

Paperback, ISBN 978-1-911077-28-2, £6.99 • ebook, ISBN 978-1-911077-29-9, £6.99